The Red Hat

The Red Hat

John Bayley

Duckworth

First published in 1997 by
Gerald Duckworth & Co. Ltd.
The Old Piano Factory
48 Hoxton Square, London N1 6PB
Tel: 0171 729 5986
Fax: 0171 729 0015

© 1997 by John Bayley

A catalogue record for this book is available
from the British Library

ISBN 0 7156 2802 X

Typeset by Ray Davies
Printed in Great Britain by
Redwood Books Ltd, Trowbridge

I

I flatter myself that I am not at all boyish, although I am often told, as if it was a compliment, that I look like a boy. 'As pretty as a boy', a gay friend with whom I am a bit in love once assured me, gazing with satisfaction at my absence of bust. I never wear a bra, I don't need to. Actually I think breasts are a bore; and the sort of men I approve of don't favour the bigger ones.

Funnily enough I used to know a splendid fellow, not at all gay, who prided himself on his own breasts. He had pectorals like a powerful fish. He once told me, too, that he could never pee in his wife's presence, but had no trouble with a girlfriend standing by. There had once been trouble about this once, and he told me why; but that, as Kipling would say – he used to be one of my favourite authors – is another story.

Peeing and all that seems suited to the Netherlands, which is where we were when this particular story happened. It's often shown in their pictures; but not, of course, in the ones by Vermeer, which we had come to see.

Why had we come? – Cloe and Charles and myself, that is. Well might one ask. I found myself wondering why after I'd been trapped for an hour or so in a small dingy room bursting with Vermeer worshippers. We weren't allowed to move until the crowd in the next room moved on; and when I tried to sneak out backwards I was stopped by the spreading arms of a burly Dutchman in a grey uniform, who was friendly but firm.

I gave up then even trying to look at the pictures – the devotees in a cluster round each made them all but invisible anyway – and I amused myself instead with a fantasy about being a painter like Hieronymus Bosch, and painting us all with nothing on, brooding away cheek by jowl over Vermeer's masterpieces as if we had been summoned to the Last Judgement.

There we would all be, in the nude, but pretending not to notice each other because of all the silent admiration that was going on. I wonder what old Bosch and Co would make of Vermeer? Probably not much.

Does it sound as if I know about art and artists? In fact I don't. Charles is the one that does. Charles, by the way, is the man who once told me that I looked as pretty as a boy. I've loved him for it ever since. Although he's about as queer as they come, and believe me I ought to know, Charles is trying pretty doggedly to be in love with Cloe, or to do his best to fall in love with her. She adores him of course. Cloe is supposed to be what we once used to call my best friend, which is one of the reasons I am here with them.

OK: another is because of Charles. Cloe knows about all that, but she doesn't let it worry her. Cloe is my best friend, yes: but actually I hate the idea of best friends. Or friends of any sort, come to think of it. What's the point of them? – why such a big idea? There are people you know, and a great many more whom you don't, and that's about it. So I feel; but I have known Cloe a long time, and always 'kept up' with her. And I'm always trying to impress Cloe. I can't help it.

Cloe's very feminine. If I'm boyish she's everything that a female is supposed to be. Pear-shaped, though her bottom's more like a toffee-apple. If a man were to put his fatherly hands on her shoulders, and I'm sure that plenty have done or wanted to do just that – she brings out their protective instincts – his rugged paws would slip down off them helplessly: just like those old Victorian climbers sliding off the icy top of Mont Blanc.

That's assuming she had nothing on, of course; but then she wouldn't have, would she? I imagine men usually look at her as if she'd nothing on, even when she's fully clad. If my little fantasy were to come true, and we were all there together in the picture gallery naked, I think it's just possible that Cloe might distract one or two of the male devotees from their Vermeer worship. Not that she's living art – far from it – but it could be that in the unusual circumstances I had in mind some art-fancier might wrench his gaze away from the paintings for a moment to take a normal interest in her.

Or maybe not. Still, enough of these frivolous thoughts. I was, and am, fond of old Cloe – can't deny that. Grateful to her too. She'll see why presently, if she cares to stick the course. And looking at pictures can be rather like reading a book, I suppose.

Meanwhile, there was Charles trying so hard to be in love with her. He being gay I suppose she represents for him the maximum challenge. To be in love with me wouldn't mean anything to him at all. After all those boys and men he's had he could do it in my arms at the drop of a hat.

Of a hat, yes. It was a hat that started the whole thing off. Not a real hat but the one in the Vermeer picture. It's the one of this girl, looking at you with very bright eyes, and wearing a red hat.

Of course I hardly saw the picture in the flesh, as it were. I shouldn't think many people did. Just a glimpse of it over heads and between arms. But this picture of the hat had been put on the entrance ticket, and I still have that. Two of them in fact. Little souvenirs. You'll see why presently.

What I see when I look at the ticket is the lips and the eyes – the teeth a bit too – all lustrous and gleaming, but at the same time pink and warm too. As if they were made of some divine marshmallow.

Amazing what Vermeer could do with paint. Especially pure plain white paint.

Or was it done by the people who restored the pictures? I've no idea; and I wonder if anyone else has, really. It's one of those things, and there are so many of them, that one doesn't know and would rather not know, like who are the men and women in the pictures, and what were they doing, and what happened to them afterwards.

If it comes to that the Dutch don't even seem to know what their own capital city is called. We call it the Hague; they call it Den Haag – fair enough. But they don't seem to be sure by any means, for on the map they decide to mark it "s Gravenhage'. This means 'the Count's Hedge', so a Dutchman told me. But, as my mother used to say, can't they make up their *mainds*?

Never mind that – back to the Red Hat. As I said, she's a girl. She's wearing ear-rings. Nice long pearly ones. She's wearing ear-rings like that – not queers' ear-rings you understand – and yet she's not a girl. She's a boy. That's obvious. At least it's obvious if you really start to think about it, so perhaps you shouldn't think about it.

But another thing that's obvious – and really obvious this time – is that she looks just like me. Or he does. I was absolutely staggered when Charles put the ticket into my hand. It was so abundantly clear who he was – or she – that neither Cloe nor Charles bothered to remark on the fact, and neither did I. They just looked at me with a knowing smile, to which I paid no attention. As the pressure of the devout mob, before and behind, propelled us into that black hole of an exhibition, Cloe did give my arm a squeeze and say: 'That was a bit of a shock for you, Nance, wasn't it?'

As soon as we got in Charles and Cloe began to wear their dedicated look, like everyone else in the crowd. One of the things this look takes for granted is that in pursuit of art the wearer would be prepared to undergo any quantity of discomfort. But there's nothing elitist about it you understand. Charles and Cloe don't think they're so very special. On the contrary, they assume we can all stand in front of old Vermeer for hours – and *all* of us with that special rapt look on our faces.

Actually people like Charles are not at all common, because in the pursuit of art he is prepared to undergo more than discomfort. Actual hardship. That's one of the things for which Cloe genuinely admires him. She wouldn't do it for herself – undergo hardship I mean – but she would for his sake. It's exasperating in her, but also lovable no doubt. Some kinds of women today know better than to identify with their man's interests – that wouldn't go with feminist correctness. Instead they have a way of becoming more him than he, if you see what I mean. More subtly, more sort of invasively, what he is, than what they are themselves. As well as being into Charles, Cloe is now into art in this sort of way too. Into Vermeer's pictures, that is.

Oh those pictures. The great thing for the devotees is that you stand there in silence. Just a bit of a hushed murmuring. Nobody says 'Oh look at the little boy or the little girl – aren't they *sweet!*' There are no little boys and little girls – none of those twee and cosy goings-on that there are in the other Dutch pictures painted at the same time. Could their absence make Vermeer, do you think, just a little bit boring? By the time you've stood and contemplated for ten minutes or so, along with all the others who are lost in contemplation? I daresay I am, or shall be, just a sentimental old maid really, but I do like a bit more life in my pictures. Very philistine of me no doubt. But in an odd way there's plenty of life in the girl, or boy, with the red hat.

The command was given and the crowd obediently moved on, bearing Charles and Cloe in its bosom. Soon they were standing four or five deep in front of that hefty woman who's pouring out the milk. Although she's built like an all-in wrestler she can only coax the thinnest possible stream of milk out of that great stone jug she's holding. Perhaps that's the great zen-like charm of the thing, but it can keep it as far as I am concerned.

I baulked. Smiling sweetly at the attendant who was trying to shoo me in with the others I slipped under his extended arm and back into the first room again. There was a moment's delightful emptiness in there before the next lot were let in. I said to the man 'I'm feeling a little faint – would you mind?' – and with true Dutch gallantry he let me sit down on a cold radiator. From there I could contemplate one of the Master's early paintings. Very unVermeer-like. Some female saint is wringing from a cloth into a basin the blood of a martyr who's just had his head cut off. You can see his head in the background still looking a little bit surprised. The rest of him, naturally enough, is quite unbothered.

I preferred this saint lady to the milkmaid. At least she's really getting somewhere, and she looks devoted and dedicated as if she's found the very job she ought to be doing.

It was a simple matter now to escape not only from Charles and Cloe but from Vermeer. The rooms hung with other pictures were empty. Hardly a viewer. The Vermeer exhibition had put poor old Rembrandt in the shade. Normally I'm not a great Rembrandt enthusiast. Nor is Charles, who like many of the experts hates pictures with what you might call a human interest. I don't mind that. I don't like him because he's such a show-off. Sometimes he's just like one of those more modern artists – or writers, come to that – who are always reminding us that they've got right away from any conventional nonsense, and are showing us reality as it really is.

All the same it was a relief, after the Vermeer worship, to have a quiet look at the big dusky – or perhaps just dirty? – canvas which shows us the boy David playing the harp to king Saul. Meek crafty very Jewish David is giving us a conspiratorial look, while Saul sits there in his tawdry robes, with a great tear at the corner of one eye. Saul looks as if he knew what trouble was all about, but wasn't expecting any from this young chap, at least not yet.

I idled on, nearly missing a small even dingier picture in a recess. A female figure beside a sort of sandy bank, with some weedy grass, and a dark round spot among the general dinginess which suggests a rabbit-hole. A rabbit-hole by Rembrandt is a nice thought somehow, particularly when

12

the subject is what you might call a classical one. The female is wearing one of those garments which in Rembrandt's version of the ancient world seem to have the sole function of slipping down round the hips, in order to leave bare a big bald wrinkled tummy. Did the Dutch and their patrons think those fat stomachs seductive? Or was it to cheer the men up when they looked at their wives, and to make them think their old Dutch must be really quite an oil painting? – 'if this is art I'd better try to like it' sort of thing?

This fat old girl has her hands chained above her head and looks fearfully uncomfortable, apart from her dressing-gown coming down. She's labelled Andromeda. I recalled that Rubens has a much jollier Andromeda, a rollicking great lady who looks as happy as the day is long to be showing off her charms to the cliff watchers. The languishing Victorian ones do look a bit nervous about the monster who's coming to eat them up; but they seem even more concerned to keep the graceful pose they've been arranged in by the painter; and like the Rubens lady they don't seem to mind being watched by the gents on the cliff-top, or rather in the picture gallery. No doubt the Victorians enjoyed a romantic marine landscape all the more if it could boast a damsel in distress, and in the nude.

But Rembrandt's woman is just having a lousy time, and was that his idea, I wonder? If so, you could say he's pulled it off by making you see that the real Andromeda must have had absolutely no fun at all, however sexy she looked to Perseus as he came to rescue her. Did Rembrandt get just a bit too cocky, though, picking a model who looks fat and forty? The poor thing's not so much pathetic as comic.

But maybe that was his idea too? Perhaps the real Andromeda, if such a person ever existed, *was* fat and forty? How can we know, at this moment in time, as they say? Losing interest in the question I wandered off to a giant canvas by a painter called Potter. Chiefly a cow and bull, though there was also an excellent frog. But I was beginning to feel bored with the whole art gallery. Hell, why had I come in the first place? Because of Charles I suppose.

I sighed. The bonds of love could be so tiresome. But bugger all that, and art too – I was a free agent, not like poor Andromeda. I'd sneak out and get myself something at the refreshment place. I'd noticed on the way in that they served smoked eel sandwiches. Trust the Dutch for something like that. The thought of a smoked eel sandwich made me wriggle with hunger pangs.

As I turned to go I noticed this very tall man who must have been standing behind me. Rather a good looker too. He himself was not looking at the pictures but at something in his hand. I saw it was the ticket to the exhibition, which had Vermeer's picture of the Red Hat girl reproduced on it.

Next moment he looked up and saw me. He started visibly. I mean he really did. I swear it. He had been gazing at the girl on the ticket, and then he looks up and sees her walking towards him, for by that time I was on my way out. There she was, in the flesh, minus the red hat of course. But you could have knocked him down with one of its red feathers.

I felt gratified of course, distinctly so. But what I really wanted was one of those eel sandwiches.

As I made my way to the buffet I pondered the question of the young person on that ticket; or in the real picture on the wall, somewhere among the crowds where she could scarcely be seen. Well, what is she really? – a boy or girl? Or is Vermeer so mystically Zen-like that it doesn't matter? Perhaps that's the answer, but I don't really think it is. I mean, everybody must be one or the other when it comes to the point, even if a great artist can't make up his mind while he's painting them.

I stopped again, to look more closely at the picture on my own ticket. The eyes – my own eyes – looked back at me. Was there a faint suggestion of blueness round the chin? If so, was it the beginnings of a beard, or the shadow cast by the red hat?

And then again, the portrait is full of shine and light. The shine on her nose – it's very definitely she this time – makes her look both charming and vulnerable because she doesn't know it's there. She's thinking instead how well she must look in the red hat she's been told to put on. Would he have the same thoughts, or would he just be wearing it as his natural right – a swashbuckling young man? He wouldn't be caring about the shine on his nose either.

There's another possibility too – maybe there are lots more. But one at least could be that she's not a model but a rather older and richer woman, the owner of the red hat, whom the artist has cunningly painted to appear younger than she was. She's having her portrait painted, in all her finery, by a respected but obscure artist, happy to earn a few guilders.

Naturally there was an interest in all this for me. And that was the astounded look on the face of the tall man, when I turned round and he looked up and saw me. Which did he think I was – boy or girl? Which would he have liked me to be? Did he have any trouble making up his mind?

I rather enjoyed imagining I now had other selves. And I enjoyed wondering which one, or some unknown one, he most went in for, since it was so obvious he was struck by the resemblance, and by my appearance. I daresay the thing I like in art galleries is watching the people. And being watched of course.

Not so Cloe and Charles. They really do look at the pictures, whereas I look at the pictures while I look at the people strolling about. But Charles and Cloe vie with each other, as well as showing off in their own style, so that they're not really much less philistine than I am. Not absolutely dedicated art-lovers, if the truth be told. *Miaow, miaow*, as my mother used to say sometimes.

As I ate my sandwich (I love smoked eel and never seem to get it in England) I pondered a bit about them. Not eels: Charles and Cloe. About Cloe more particularly. Was it she who had wanted me with them on this trip? Or had it been Charles? Which of my selves had they fancied might be useful, or reassuring – someone to distract them from each other? They're the kind of couple who find it easier to be on good terms with each other if a third party is present. I've noticed that's not uncommon even with a pair who've been married for years. They need another person to show off their close and harmonious relationship, particularly if its closeness and harmony consists in bickering all the time.

Married couples are gruesome; but, mind you, anyone can see that Cloe will be just right for the job, in time. Meanwhile she's one of those women who can only be sure they exist if they identify with someone else's existence. Touching really – or is it? Of course whatever oaf she attaches herself to takes it as no more than his due. And both she and the oaf – Charles in this case – want someone else, like me, to be the witness, and the guarantee, so to speak, of their existence as a couple.

It's not the first time it's happened to me, and it probably won't be the last.

Finishing my sandwich I decided I couldn't struggle back inside. I assumed Cloe and Charles would realise I had gone back to the hotel, and that is what I did. Now comes the first surprise.

It wasn't a bad hotel at all. Nice and oldfashioned, but at the same time up to the minute: they didn't give you a key for your bedroom door, but a dinky little bit of plastic that looked like a domino counter. I had been amused at first by the way it wouldn't work, whichever way round you put it, until you took it out and put it in the other way. Made it more human somehow. Perhaps the lock had to read it first, like an old porter peering out of a cubbyhole, before it was prepared to open up? I had plenty of time to think about that plastic key later on, because it's very far from being another story.

I walked past the bar, which was also oldfashioned, but I

felt no inclination to go in. Up to a point I quite like to drink, but if I'm on my own I'd rather do it in private. There's something so dreary about the way you get looked at in those places – particularly by single men, or women – and equally dreary is the nonchalant way you avoid looking back at them. It often makes me think that sex, like drinking, is something best done on one's own.

My single room was on the top floor. There was a lift of course, and it was a real oddity, although you could call it a part of the oldfashioned charm. Charles, who is no great shakes as a man of action and resource, pretended when we first arrived that he was afraid of it. Perhaps he really was? He and Cloe used to get out on the first floor to go to their room, and leave me to trundle on up to the top. For a lift it was enormous, like a small room itself, and it seemed to be of irregular shape. There was a comfortable chair in one corner. And there were no doors on either side. You just got out when it stopped, and a carpeted landing appeared on one side or the other, down which you proceeded to your numbered accommodation. Certainly a rum sort of lift; I should think an heirloom from the early days of technology. Lifts were made then to look like rooms I expect, as cars started off by looking like carriages. No doubt the hotel was very proud of it.

It was at the end of a little lobby, open and welcoming and lit up inside, rather like a Vermeer interior come to think of it – perhaps that was the idea? – and as I walked in I saw there was a man sitting on the chair in the corner. He was dark-suited, and his head was bowed forward a good bit, as if in pain, or perhaps in meditation. I wondered if there was usually a lift operator, to go with the ancient conveyance, and if so this might be the chap, having a quiet kip in the absence of custom.

But perhaps he was a hotel guest like myself? Anyway I automatically remarked 'Oh sorry,' as one does by reflex in

England in almost any situation. Funnily enough the Dutch use the word too.

The man did not reply, neither did he look up. With a sort of inner gulp of vulgar excitement I thought he might have had a heart attack in the lift, sat down and died. Or perhaps it was a Vermeerish murder, very unsensational, commonplace, and yet quietly mysterious of course? Perhaps he had a dagger handle between his dark-clad shoulder-blades?

These childish speculations were put a stop to in a very peculiar way. I had gone over to the dashboard, as you might call it, where the would-be lift traveller pressed numbered buttons in order to rise to his or her floor. As my finger approached Number 4 – I had assumed by now that I had better take no notice of the man in the armchair – I became conscious that the lift had already started to move, though it was hard to say in which direction. At the same moment two hands, dark and hairy, took hold of me by the waist, either side, and gently pulled me astraddle on to the seated man's knees, face to face with him.

I was so astonished that I just sat there, not uncomfortably. And now that I was looking into his face, which was big dark and handsome like the rest of him, I realised that he was the man in the museum, the man who had been looking at the picture of the Red Hat on his ticket, and who had given such a start when he saw me walking towards him.

Well! I had certainly made an impression, and every girl, or even boy-girl, likes to do that I suppose. In a curious way it was so peaceful just to sit astride him and gaze into his face, which was kindly and relaxed, that I began to feel we were a kind of Vermeer couple – one had the painter on the brain of course – as if he were about to teach me some instrument like the virginals, which happened to require a certain amount of close proximity for its operation. Sitting on the other fellow's saddle, as you might say. At any rate I wasn't conscious of his cock, though it must have been just under my crotch, and in spite of my astonishment I found

18

myself smiling into his peaceable face in the solicitous and slightly apologetic way in which one smiles at a handicapped person. Perhaps he was paralysed from the waist down? But as an old masterhand on the virginals, or whatever they might be, he liked sometimes to share his expertise with a young disciple, as best he could?

So we sat a minute or so in silence, and a minute's a long time in a lift, that I can tell you. His eyes were expressionless, but seemed full of friendly goodwill. Not surprising perhaps if this was what he had been wanting to do, and now he was doing it. His eyes didn't exactly devour me, but they had the impersonal concentration which one has when looking at a picture which really appeals, rather than one which we all know we must stand in front of and look at a long time. I've noticed that us ordinary folk, as opposed to the Charleses of the art world, only look at a picture in the way I mean when there's something in it which appeals personally and privately; and for obvious reasons that often means something to do with sex.

So how much longer was I going to sit on his knees there, as if I were riding a cock-horse to Banbury Cross? Perhaps Balthus ought to have come along and painted us, although I would resent any suggestion that I look like a Balthus girl – I don't at all. Was the man going to carry matters further? Start doing something else? I didn't feel particularly perturbed about that. Things were too quiet and peaceful, as if the Red Hat girl had indeed strayed into the room where a well-dressed man – Vermeer's fellows are all well-dressed of course – is giving the young lady the lesson on the virginals. I reflected anyway, as moments calmly passed, that as things stood there was a sufficiency of material obstacles – his trousers and mine, two pairs of pants, our shirt-ends as well, between me and trouble. That is if he were to start anything else, which at the moment he gave absolutely no sign of doing.

I detest jeans: all girls wear them. I get my trousers made

for me by a proper tailor, though I don't go so far as to have a zip put in at the front. At the side it makes a better fit. I have them done in tweed, or a nice woollen material, or sometimes in that ski-pant stuff, though I don't go for it much – too modern and flashy. My present pair were a choice herringbone pattern, in sober shades of grey. I admit I did idly reflect, while seated there, that it might be just as well there was no front zip.

So we sat. It was getting a bit timeless, like a picture, and the lift was motionless now of course. I had the feeling it had come to rest at the bottom. The apertures at the side were blank – one had something stencilled on it in Dutch – and somewhere behind it there were subdued sounds of activity, a rattle of plates and occasional voices. But it seemed clear there was no way in or out at the sides, and that was why we were here. Like being in a tube train that stops between the stations.

At last – it felt like that but had probably been less than two minutes – he lifted me carefully off his knees and set me on my feet. Turning away, he pressed a button I suppose. We rose up in a leisurely way, and soon there was a melodious clang like a ship's telegraph and a light came on the 4 sign. We had arrived, and there was my carpeted corridor stretching away, and looking all lit-up and warm. I stepped out, looked back with a smile, and said 'Thank you'. That was all there was to it. As I looked back I had a glimpse of him, very tall and black he looked, standing as it were officially by the control panel. Perhaps he really is the liftman I thought, repressing an impulse to wave.

As I walked down the passage I realised I was carrying the little domino plastic thing in my hand. I must have taken it out of my bag as I walked into the lift, and sat there with it throughout the curious episode that followed. Somehow it must have completed the picture, I thought, had any old master been there to paint it; and viewers afterwards might have peered a bit as they said: 'What's that funny little thing she's got in her hand?'

I enjoyed a bath, and put on my usual clothes, just as I had been in the lift. I wanted to do that somehow, for the lift was a happy memory. There had been nothing much to it, certainly no sex, at least not for me, but there had been an odd feeling of kindness about the encounter. I really felt as if something worthwhile had happened; and I had warm feelings towards the lift man, if that was what he was, without any wish to see him again.

Indeed I rather consciously hoped that he wouldn't be there in the lift when I went down to Charles and Cloe's room. A bit apprehensive about what might happen a second time. But I needn't have worried. He wasn't. Charles and Cloe were in the bar, and full of Vermeer of course: though being the sort of *real* picture people they – or at least Cloe – set out to be, they didn't gush at all, or say anything indicating the commoner kinds of enthusiasm.

They made comments on my absence, naturally. I fully expected that.

'Of course, my dear Nance,' said Charles, 'you feel that you don't need to see the collection, as we ordinary people do. You so obviously already belong to it yourself.'

I didn't take the trouble to answer him. I smiled sweetly and said nothing. Charles's malice never bothers me at all. I find it a kind of compliment, and it could be one of the reasons why I love him. If I do love him. In my own sort of way – and his I think – we did at that moment. I wrinkled up my nose at him and we grinned privately at each other. For a second or two it was rather bliss.

'You can instruct me at the virginals some time,' I told him. 'The gentleman who's been supervising me is not really my type.'

Cloe intervened, but careful not to be cross. 'When you two have quite finished,' she said, 'perhaps Charles would like to bend his mind to the question of our dinner. I'm starving.'

'I'm not,' I said. 'I had an eel sandwich – delicious' – and I wriggled my fingers at them.

Cloe pretended to look disgusted, and then yawned rather offensively. 'Don't flaunt your eels at me, Nancy-boy,' she said. 'We don't want to hear, do we Charles, what the creature gets up to when art isn't good enough for her.'

Of course I had no intention of telling them about the lift. That was my own private experience, when I had my red hat on, so to speak. I enjoyed smiling at them and thinking about it though.

Cloe had changed into a black silk moiré evening skirt, which distinctly suited her. She and Charles were drinking glasses of white wine. They didn't suggest getting one for me, and I didn't want one anyway. There always seems to be far too much white wine about nowadays.

I was prepared to sit patiently. I knew they wouldn't want to dine at the hotel. They're the sort who when travelling always think there must be a much more interesting little place to have dinner round the corner somewhere. Quite often, of course, they're right about that. Hotel dinners are usually dull and insipid, and the dining-room apt to be full of old people who look at you in a depressing way. At the same time Charles and Cloe make a point of going out that's rather tiresome, as if they owed it to themselves as lively young persons. They're not particularly young actually, and lively? – well, in a rather obligatory way, like some duty that's taken for granted.

We wandered round the streets in a drizzle that made a mild hissing noise as it hit the surface of a canal. Charles rejected one nice-looking little place because it was too crowded, another because it looked suspiciously empty, a third because the menu outside didn't feature dishes he liked, or at least the sort of things he felt one ought to eat in Holland. It seemed a long time now since my eel sandwich.

22

Cloe was predictably stoical. Being in love with Charles she knew better than to complain, and besides she's phlegmatic by nature. Being the shape she is she's clearly got a bigger hunger threshold than I have.

At last we found a little place that called itself an Israeli restaurant. Charles and Cloe were charmed. Perhaps the drizzle by now had something to do with that. We'd passed a couple of Indonesian places which Charles felt – quite wrongly I'm sure – were not the proper places to go when in the Hague. Was Israeli food the same as Jewish, he now wondered, as we stood there in the rain. As it had now come on quite heavily even his exasperating powers of procrastination were at last overcome. In we went.

There were only four or five tables, all empty. We sat down at one of them. There was a bar, with a couple of people standing at it who might have been either guests or waiters. They did not seem pleased to see us and paid us no attention, continuing to talk among themselves in a language which could have been Dutch but probably wasn't. That put Charles on his mettle, and after a moment or two he went up rather aggressively to the bar and asked for the menu.

I could see that this provoked an unhelpful response. There wasn't one, evidently; and a tall athletic fellow behind the bar could be heard explaining to Charles in very reasonable English that there was a dish of the day. He seemed to imply that they had nothing but contempt for the fawning decadent ways of a bourgeois restaurant. Their image was a simple heroic one, as on a kibbutz; and casual visitors were expected to be rather thrilled by it, and also made to feel a bit small.

Charles appeared to come to an agreement with the barman, and returned to our table to tell us, with a certain self-satisfaction, that we were to have hors d'oeuvres Haifa-style, with lamb chops and chips to follow.

That sounded all right, except that it wasn't. The hors

d'oeuvres were stale pitta with vinegary houmous, and a sort of ghastly red paste, and the chops were far too tough to eat. We sat gloomily masticating chips, and Charles got all bright and defensive, praising the Mount Carmel wine, which was not disagreeable but seemed barely alcoholic.

It was definitely diuretic, however, and just as we were about to leave I decided to go to the Ladies. There was a door I could see with the male logo on it – the forked-looking object – but no sign of the trim lady in her skirt. Was it a unisex toilet? Or were only those bursting with virility entitled to patronise it? Provoked, I was about to push the door open when I noticed another one, unlabelled, in the alcove beside it. So I tried that instead.

Two men were sitting in there at a small table under a light. One was the athletic-looking type from the bar, and the other was small and slight, with a white face and a dark moustache. His bright black eyes looked up and gazed into mine, and I found myself momentarily hypnotised and unable to do anything but stare back at him.

It was a long moment, but then I muttered the usual 'Sorry' – that so handy Dutch-English – shut the door and went back to our table. After those eyes I didn't have the nerve somehow to try the one with the Gents sign: I would just have to wait now till we got back to our hotel. Cloe raised her eyebrows in a feminine query, to intimate that she might follow me if I had been successful, so I smiled at her in the same spirit. In sheer desperation we had drunk three bottles of that Mount Carmel stuff.

'The non-Gents is full of gents,' I told her cryptically. I rather liked to think of me and Cloe at that moment as both looking like the trim logo lady in her skirt. Demure and slightly disdainful. Not like the forked male.

Charles meanwhile ignored us, for he was absorbed in working out sums in guilders. He had been sternly told they didn't take credit cards, and this had thrown him somewhat. Dutch currency is rather pretty in its way, and has a tremendously *caring* look. Emphatically designed to be used by the halt, the lame and the blind.

I noticed the bright red and green notes mechanically, as Charles was fussing with them, but really I had had rather a shock. I kept seeing the small white face, and the black eyes looking squarely into mine across the table. The big bronzed Israeli with him was obviously a subordinate, though he had not himself bothered with our dinner at all – that had been done by a silent sour-faced girl who brought it from somewhere at the back of the bar and dumped it in front of us.

Back at the hotel I was still feeling puzzled. Baffled rather. There was something about that face. I knew I had seen it before; and yet where could I have seen it?

After I came out of the Ladies – a real Ladies with paper towels and toilet water – I found Charles and Cloe being very animated at the reception desk, over the great question of tickets. They were busy getting the ones for our ration of Vermeer-viewing, next day; and wondering in loud voices what times would be the most strategic for squeezing in an extra hour. The people at the reception desk smiled tolerantly, pleased to think the English rude and childish, not like good Dutch children. They were also asking if we wanted tickets for the big dance at the town hall tomorrow evening. They showed us the poster, decorated inevitably by a picture of the girl in the red hat. They looked at me knowingly and said it was a fancy dress dance: many people would be got up as some character out of Vermeer. Cloe decided of course that we must go.

'You've got it made, Nance,' she pointed out. 'We'll just have to find you the right hat.' Girls like Cloe can never resist the obvious.

They went into the bar, and I decided to go up to bed. The lift seemed an old friend by now, and as I entered it of course I wondered where the man was who had sat me on his knees, and if he were still hanging about. What an odd kind of charm he had, or so it seemed to me now. I had been too surprised at the time to have really taken it in.

I was woken some time in the night by a faint scratching sound. They say, don't they, that a noise like that is more likely to wake you up than a much louder one? Then I heard the door of the bedroom, which was down one of those little passages with a loo and a cupboard off it, being quietly opened. There was no time to do anything about it, even if I had been wide enough awake to put two and two together. There was a rustling sound quite close, and someone got into bed with me.

I knew it was a man of course. It sort of smelled like a man, and though I wouldn't put it past Cloe to have Lesbian tendencies, and even to act on them where I was concerned, it seemed highly unlikely none the less that she would have abandoned Charles in quest of me. Besides, how would she have got in? The locks on the doors closed automatically.

I had time to think of these things and several others, and also to wonder what to do. It should have been a panic situation, but for some reason it wasn't. I should have screamed, fumbled for the light, shot out of the bed on the opposite side. I did none of these things. Was it because I sort of knew, though almost unconsciously, who this man was?

It was pitch dark of course – just the vaguest bit of light from the window area. For a single the bed was reasonably large, and he didn't touch me, except that our feet gently collided. His were nice and warm.

I addressed the darkness boldly, which seemed after a second or two the best idea. 'How did you get in?' I asked.

A voice replied that it had been quite easy. In the lift he hadn't spoken, but he had just the kind of voice I would have expected: foreign but pleasantly foreign, deep and slightly husky.

It amused me to realise, when I heard it, that if it had turned out to be one of those upper-class standard English voices I *should* have leaped out of the bed pretty smartish, telling the invisible man, in the same sort of tones, to get the hell out of it.

Perhaps the man could tell now that I was smiling in the dark, although I have to admit that I was also beginning to feel more than a trifle fluttery. I had been sitting on his knee in the lift fully clad, and in my substantial trousers, and here I was in bed with nothing on. I never wear anything in bed, not for any erotic reason but because I find it more comfortable that way.

But how had he got in? I was about to ask again when I remembered that when I was sitting on his knee in the lift I must have been holding the plastic key thing in my hand. Could there be some connection?

Apparently there could. Still without touching me he began quietly and laboriously to explain that he had a photographic memory. He memorised the location of the holes in my card, and as he had key blanks and a proper punch it was no trouble to make a card of his own. I found his voice irresistible. It was calm and low and slightly husky. Courteous, but quite unapologetic.

He came three times before it began to get light. No apology for it either. Once he tried to do it to me the other way round, but I wasn't having any of that. I'm not a boy after all, and there's Aids to think of, even at a moment when I was beginning to be half in love with my liftman, as I still thought of him. This dark gentle foreigner who had got into bed with me, and who spoke with such a lovely unEnglish voice.

He left me about six, as quietly as he had arrived. We had very little conversation, apart from the bed sort. To tease him I asked him once if he was doing all right. He picked up the tease – it was just before the third lovemaking – and told me with a little chuckle that he would be in a moment. As he slipped out of bed he murmured in his funny voice what sounded like 'You a good lad – a smart lad.' I didn't grasp the words at once, but they started me off giggling after the door closed.

I'd felt him carefully at first to make sure he was using a condom; and he'd been very meticulous about using a new one each time. I found he'd put them tidily on a sheet of hotel stationery beside the bed. I popped them in one of those little sanitary bags they give you in the loo, printed with a lady wearing a bouffant skirt, and looking for some reason much more rackety than the self-possessed lady on the toilet door. The chambermaid was hardly likely to investigate it, and I have some solicitude for the drains in hotel bedrooms, having once found that I'd been given a blocked one. Naturally enough they're not like ordinary drains, with a short urethra, so to speak. They must wind about from room to room.

He had been thoughtful in his precautions. But naturally he was protecting himself too, which he obviously needed to if he did this kind of thing often. Somehow, though, I didn't feel that he did. That was sentimental of me no doubt. But I was a bit in love, or rather, to be honest, just feeling pleased with myself.

Why was that? Partly because he had called me a smart lad; and partly because I was sure that he had very much enjoyed himself. Partly, too, for the much odder reason that there had been no sex in it for me, or only the barest minimum, and I'm usually quite a sexy sort of person. But he hadn't turned me on at all, and I felt mysteriously gratified by that. Rather maternal I suppose. And although he'd kept me awake about four hours, and had hardly said anything, I hadn't been in the least bored. Quite the contrary.

I'd arranged to meet with Cloe and Charles at eight for breakfast, since we had to report early with our tickets at the Mauritshuis Museum. If it hadn't been for Vermeer the amorous couple would no doubt have had their *petit déjeuner* snugly upstairs in their room. I always like to come down myself, in any hotel, and whether I'm alone or not. No *petit déjeuner* stuff for me. I like to confront whatever there is going, although at home I admit I never much care for the sound of a 'full English breakfast'. But the Dutch do it admirably. Everything from Gouda to frankfurters and from radishes to kiwi fruit.

Cloe watched me tucking in with a look that was half indulgent and half envious. She knows she'll get fat and she knows that I won't. But she took a sort of pride, all the same, in my plateful of goodies, as if I were her little boy. I was touched by this. Charles of course paid us no attention. He drank a lot of coffee, ate a brioche, and pretended to read a Dutch newspaper. Occasionally, to keep us amused, he mouthed bits at us: but *sotto voce*, in case there was a real Dutchman within earshot.

It was while he was doing this that the penny suddenly dropped. I was pretending to laugh at Charles's performance as a Dutchman when I caught sight of the photographs on the front page of his paper – Arab looking characters, some in headscarves and some without. At once I remembered the man who had been in the room last night at the restaurant, when I opened the door thinking it might be the Ladies. And I knew where I'd seen him before. It was on the front page of a newspaper, back in England. It was a picture of some notorious terrorist from the Middle East, who was suspected of being behind the latest atrocity. I couldn't remember which it was or where: there are so many of them.

Anyway, that was the man I had seen in the restaurant. Looking at the pictures in Charles's paper made me suddenly quite sure of it. With hindsight I now feel I could easily have been wrong – they are all apt to look so alike in a spruce expressionless way – but that kind of uncertainty was to become typical of our whole Dutch adventure. Just as you don't know who the people are in those Vermeer pictures, or what they are thinking about and doing. Charles would no doubt say I've got that all wrong too, and very likely I have.

My conviction, at least at that moment, was that the man I had seen in the restaurant was the famous terrorist. I felt quite thrilled at the thought, but I didn't say anything. What could the man be doing there, in a so-called Israeli restaurant? The whole thing was so inexplicable that I soon ceased to think about it, in the way one does about funny coincidences to which one will never discover the answer, if it exists.

I started to think instead about my companion of the night. There had been nothing unreal about him, and the thought of him soon gave me that nice warm feeling again. Who on earth was he, who could he be? But that didn't really worry me particularly. Whoever he was, he had a thing about me; and perhaps I should see him again. Perhaps tonight he'd be getting back in bed with me? And perhaps tonight I'd be really passionate and abandoned.

I toyed with the idea that it would have been nice to have him come down to breakfast with me. Wouldn't Charles and Cloe have looked surprised? But I soon dropped that notion, amusing as it was to think of. My man of the night, and of the lift of course, was my own private property; and I wasn't going to mix him up, or let him have anything to do with Charles and Cloe. Or with anyone else at the hotel for that matter.

*

Our morning viewing was over at last; and looking more goofy than ever Charles and Cloe allowed themselves to be herded with the others to the exit. Hours had passed, or seemed to have passed, and as we filtered out through the giant queue waiting to come in I began to think again about an eel sandwich. No chance of that. Cloe was too intent on pressing on now to the shops to buy things for the dance at the town hall; but when the pair of them stopped on a street corner to debate the best way to go, with Charles making quite a good shot at playing the obliging husband, I seized the chance of buying and eating a *maatje*. These are a delicious chunk of raw herring, which you get with onion inside a roll. When they saw me eating it the lovers turned away without comment. Perhaps the sight was too much for their sensibilities. Perhaps because it made them both feel hungry.

Women going purposefully into shops – real women – resemble the Will in Action. Cloe tore into them, hurling things about and throwing them back on the counter, while the shop people watched her indulgently. They always appreciate a passionate seeker, and the placid Dutch assistants were quite galvanised by her energies. She was quick too – I will say that. In no time we were all more or less kitted out for the evening do: Charles as the obvious cavalier, and Cloe as the wax-faced beauty holding a wineglass.

I suspect that Cloe might like to have gone as the much better-known girl – the slack-jawed pop-eyed one with the turban tassel and the pearl ear-ring – who is gazing moonily over her own shoulder. Cloe could actually look like this girl although the girl doesn't look like her, if that makes any sense. Probably it doesn't. But a wise woman knows her own limitations, and there's nothing unwise about Cloe. She knows she's not mysterious, and the girl with the turban is so banal that she manages to be mysterious. If she were a bright girl there would be no mystery at all. And Cloe's a perfectly bright girl.

She didn't bother much with her own costume. She bought a couple of yards of dark material to drape across Charles's bosom, but chiefly she was determined to get me my red hat.

And this turned out to be a hard job. Whether the good folk of the Hague had bought up all the hats they could find, in expectation of going in fancy dress to the ball, or whether hats of all sorts are now so much in short supply, there was scarcely a hat to be found in the town, least of all a red one. But Cloe ought to have been christened Determination, as girls used to be called Modesty or Prudence. There are a lot of old clothes and antiques and charity shops in the old part of the town by the canals, and Cloe dragged me into every last one of them. Charles had gone back to the hotel by now of course, leaving the girls to it.

In the grubbiest of all the shops, kept by an old crone of a Dutch lady who would have made a strong appeal as a model to Metsu or even Rembrandt, Determination-Cloe unearthed a tatty old headdress made of what appeared to be ostrich feathers. It was grey with dirt, and so full of dust and dead moths that the crone went to shake it out in the canal. She let us have it for a guilder. I pointed out that I'd have to go as the Girl in a Dirty Off-white Hat. Cloe, however, said she could fix that. She sounded mysterious, and pleased with herself of course, but Cloe is certainly a great fixer, just as she can drive a hard bargain. It takes a girl who looks as alluringly helpless as she does to be really good at that sort of thing.

She was as good as her word. She shooed Charles out of their room, and me too. He wanted me to come with him to find a marine panorama done as a kind of gigantic *trompe l'oeil* by some nineteenth-century Dutch painter called Mesdag or something. One of the sights of the Hague, so the guidebook said. Charles, the Vermeer buff, looked a little hangdog at wanting to visit such a commonplace attraction; and I felt touched by this and nearly agreed to go. I was sort of in love with him after all. But honestly, after that morning at the Mauritshuis I didn't feel I could face any more artists, even a nice vulgar Victorian one. I told Charles I'd rather kick stones about in the square outside our hotel, so he went off sulkily by himself.

The odd one out, and the useless one, as not seldom happens to me, I really did feel rather like kicking a stone. So I walked about the square and surreptitiously kicked one or two of the crocuses instead. They were arranged to give a Mondrian effect, in irregular shapes and blocks of white and mauves, sometimes with an orange or a dark purple line running diagonally between them. Very tasteful. I thought about the man whose picture had been in the papers. I was still sure that he had been the same man I saw when I opened the door which should have been the Ladies.

But I couldn't feel interest in that any more. It often seems to be the case that the oddest things that happen to one in life are also the most boring. Too inexplicable to be any real fun; and not mystical and enigmatic like you know who. Chaps like Vermeer, that is. But of course this wasn't true of my man of the night, my liftman. Thinking of him could still give me that warm feeling.

Where was he now, and what was he doing? I should never find out probably, just as I should never know about the man in what should have been the Ladies, with the white face and black moustache. My man was quite different of course. And yet, like the other one, I felt I should never see him again, or find out where he'd come from. I didn't feel sad about this, as I roamed around the square by the hotel. It seemed somehow inevitable. It doesn't occur to one to worry, after all, about the fact that one will never see again the people in the street, or in a hotel, or an art gallery, just as one will never know what happened afterward to the people in Vermeer's pictures.

Even so, when Cloe rang my room at six 'clock, and told me to come down and get dressed up, I couldn't help having the faint hope that my man of the night might be sitting in the corner of the lift. Of course he wasn't, and in one way I was almost glad. I'd had my adventure. He must have been a fellow guest, on the wing as it were, who'd seen me, and fancied me.

No doubt he'd left the hotel early. He couldn't be sure, after all, that I wouldn't make a fuss of some sort when I'd got over the excitement, so to speak, and thought about it in cold blood, in the morning.

He needn't have worried; but how was he to know that, even though I felt he knew me pretty well? As I went down in the lift another part of me felt a pang. I felt I had amused

33

him in some way; and it was his amusement at me that I was half in love with, I think. I had made him laugh: indeed the clearest thing I remembered about him was that low chuckle he'd given in the night when I asked him, ironically, if he was having a nice time. He'd muttered in my ear something that sounded like 'Oh ho boy'. It sounded so sincere somehow. Something about me had made him laugh. And I had been his boy, at least for the night.

He certainly needn't have worried that I might complain to the management in the morning.

Cloe had worked like a black. I believe they used to say such things, before these PC times. She'd worked like a black, and produced a red hat.

How had she done it? I remembered she'd dived in to a chemist's shop on the way back, and wouldn't let me come with her. I assumed she was being coy for some reason and needed to buy contraceptives or tampons. She'd wanted it to be a surprise she now told me, bringing out from the bathroom a marvellous red ostrich feather headdress.

I mean, the transformation was really astonishing! First she'd washed and combed the grotty old thing as if it were the head of John the Baptist. Then with the red dye she'd bought at the chemist she'd dyed it in the basin. Finally, she told me, she'd blown it dry with the electric hairdrier in the bathroom. And there it was.

Charles had arrived by now. Very carefully Cloe fixed the red hat on my head, and both of them stood back to admire it. Cloe literally clapped her hands. She had created me, she felt: she could see her creation as a catalogue item, No. 14 in the little booklet we had been given with the tickets. Number 14. The Girl with the Red Hat, c. 1665. National Gallery of Art, Washington. On loan to the Mauritshuis for the exhibition. Looking at me from a distance, with her own head thrown back, Cloe was experiencing the satisfaction of an artist.

It didn't last, of course – I daresay it never does. In a

minute or two she had the hat off me and was bustling about with something else. Out of the hotel's pillowslip she had made herself a sort of Dutch cap, with hanging white wings. Very becoming it was. There was a steeple hat for Charles, in cardboard, with a piece of the black cloth she'd bought glued over it. Cloe had borrowed a big wineglass from the bar which she could hold up to her face from time to time as in the picture – Number 6. The Girl with the Wineglass – and which helped to give her that clueless and obliging look.

They made me take off my shirt and trousers and put on Charles's blue silk dressing gown, with tights under it of course. Then we were ready to go.

I caught sight of myself in a big mirror as we went down the stairs, and was, I admit, quite impressed. So were the Dutch ladies sitting in the lounge. They smiled; their voices rose; and they pointed out my hat to one another with little moos and coos of amazement. They even gave us a decorous clap as we went past. Cloe smirked a bit, as well she might.

It's not uncommon in social life, at least in my experience, that the high spot of the evening comes much too early. That was it, so far as I was concerned. As soon as we got out of the taxi at the Town Hall I knew it was going to be pretty awful, and I could see that Charles and Cloe thought so too. But with those two you never know. A lot of people can look absolutely fed up and miserable at the start of a jolly party, and become more riotous than anyone before it's over. I felt in their case that might be what was going to happen.

Nor was I wrong. In any case the Dutch do these things better than we would. In the tradition of *kermesse*, or what-ever they call it, their placidity becomes a kind of frenzy. A huge Dutchman seized Cloe at once, and Charles danced with me for a moment or two as if he felt he ought to be protective. Then he rushed off to rescue Cloe, and the pair of them soon disappeared into the crowd. I stood on the side-lines a bit, and tried to look as if I was quite happy to be smiling with my bright eyes, as in the picture, and wearing my red hat. Actually I had to peer under those ostrich feathers just as the person – girl or boy – in the picture is doing.

Girl or Boy? Perhaps that was the trouble? I daresay the Dutch are really very decorous, in spite of Amsterdam and drugs and all that, and like to know where they are about these things. Was I a boy dressed up as a girl? Would any boor (I use the word in a technical, not an offensive sense) who asked me to dance risk being uproariously teased by his uncouth companions? From where I stood the floor and the assembly in general looked overpoweringly heterosexual. No gay element was visible at all. People were hanging blearily on to the brass rail of the big bar. All the makings of a genre drinking scene.

At that moment Charles suddenly reappeared at my elbow, rather to my relief. He looked as if he'd already got hold of a good deal to drink. Pressing me closely against himself he rushed me into the dance, which was quite wild by that time. He seemed highly pleased with himself, and determined to show how masterful he could be.

'You look like the duck-rabbit,' he said, leering at me and giving me a kiss on the mouth. He smelt strongly of gin. I leaned my head back from him in a rather Victorian way.

'How so?' I asked, not in the least wanting to know. 'You'll have to explain.'

'It was an experiment by Freud, or one of his disciples. Some of his patients thought a shadow model looked like a duck; some saw it as a rabbit.'

'And where do I come in?'

'Don't be so coy, or so obtuse. Some see you as one thing, some as another. But I like you as the painting, which is neither girl nor boy. Most good artists – Velasquez for instance – *place* their sitters, once and for all. The portrait tells us what they are, and that's it. But nobody knows what Vermeer's sitters were like, and especially not you, the Red Hat person.'

'Well thanks very much,' I said, to shut him up. When

Charles does start to hold forth on art it is difficult to stop him, and of course the drink made him worse than usual. But as we staggered about, for that is that it must have looked like, as I couldn't be bothered to try to lead him, I became aware that we had attracted the attention of a lot of the Dutch revellers. They converged on us, also staggering a bit. Perhaps the sight of me in Charles's arms had released whatever doubts and inhibitions they had begun by feeling about me.

Suddenly two or three of them swooped down and I was borne away. They twirled me round between them, the blue dressing gown swung upwards, and there I was from the waist down in my tights. There were grunts, whistles and mooings: not so much of admiration, probably, as of gratification that my sex at least had been confirmed. In a few seconds I had quite a gang round me, pulling me this way and that. Not men only either. It was the women – bull-like *vrows* or whatever they call them in Dutch – who were doing it as much as the men.

It was all becoming rather annoying, and I was losing my cool a bit, when who should I suddenly spot but my friend of the night, standing over near the doorway. I was amazed, as well as relieved, for something in me at once took it for granted that he was there to rescue a damsel in distress. And yet I felt disappointed too. I didn't want to see him here; in fact I don't think I really wanted to see him again at all.

But there he was anyway, unmistakably. He was so tall that his head and shoulders were clear of the excited mob, who were whooping away now and knocking coloured balloons about above their heads. Some of them pinched and fondled me as I wriggled through the dense crowd until I got up to the door.

'Am I glad to see you,' I told him. 'You can protect me against this lot. They've poked me black and blue.'

'I'll dance with you if you like,' I added. As I looked up at his face I realised rather abruptly that if I hadn't at all wanted to see him, he very much more hadn't wanted to see me. Oh dear. I could hear my voice trail away uncertainly. It had been quite the wrong suggestion to make.

There was no doubt that he found it unseemly too, as well as untimely. He gazed right over my head, looking embarrassed.

'That is not right with my job just now,' he said, in decidedly frosty tones. He seemed as indifferent to my chagrin as he had been to my surprise. I wondered how long ago he had seen me during the festivities. Dancing with Charles? Being pulled about by the jolly Dutch crowd?

'So what is your job?' I asked him, trying to re-establish myself. 'Are you the doorman?'

To my surprise he looked relieved at that, as if I were talking sense at last.

'I am a policeman,' he said.

I gaped at him. He had defined himself. Like what Charles had said about a portrait by Velasquez or someone. And now that I really looked at him, standing head and shoulders above the crowd, I realised what else could he possibly be but a policeman? He was no longer my man of the night. Had he managed it all – being in the lift, appearing in the darkness in my room – simply by being a policeman?

At that moment – trust her – Cloe suddenly arrived. She rushed at us across the floor, the wings of her white bonnet floating wildly. She halted herself prettily, as if about to curtsey, and gave my policeman – I should have to call him that to myself now – an up-from-under look. I ground my teeth.

I mean I didn't really. But Cloe is too maddening. Gazing up at my policeman she looked up as if she was going to put a thumb in her pretty mouth and start sucking it. Instead she gave a little tinkle of a laugh, and I realised that Cloe too had got hold of a good deal to drink, probably out of the same bottle as Charles.

'Oh but sorry. I mustn't interrupt,' she said, and rushed

away as attractively and tempestuously as she had come. My policeman gazed after her.

At that moment Charles chose to arrive. He would too, wouldn't he? Ignoring the policeman he made another effort to carry me off for dancing purposes, gripping me like a drowning sailor. Actually more like a drunken octopus. He seemed to have hands everywhere but no feet at all.

We trundled about like that for a minute or two, with me now trying to release myself and go back to my policeman. I suddenly, and very strongly, did want to see him and be with him, even if he took no notice of me; and here was this oaf Charles holding me so tight I could hardly breathe. I hated my policeman seeing me like this with Charles. Freeing my hands with an effort I gave him a violent push in the chest that nearly knocked him over.

I was just about to turn and run back to where my policeman had stood when a great mob of young Dutch persons, Cloe borne among them like a nymph among satyrs, came tearing down on us again. With a whoop Cloe seized me with both hands, not by the waist but by the hat. She had my lovely red hat off my head in an instant, and stuck it on her own.

The Dutch crowd applauded, at least I suppose that was what was signified by the noise they made. Furious, I tried to grab my hat back, but with shrieks and laughter they stopped me, and Cloe produced the pillowcase bonnet with strings that she'd been wearing, and jammed it down on my head, wrong way round. I was livid. I'd have scratched her face if I could have got at her. At least that is what angry women are – or were – supposed to do: and I felt very much an angry woman at that moment.

By the time I got the bonnet thing off my head and out of my eyes they had all rushed away again, still bearing Cloe like a captive or a mascot, and I saw her blonde head with the red hat on it vanish out of the door. Bleary Charles caught hold of me again, and now I hardly cared. It crossed my mind to wonder whether Cloe had made that Maenad rush at us to rescue Charles from my embraces? Had she stolen the red hat she'd made for me so carefully out of jealousy and resentment?

The thought cheered me up a trifle as I swung listlessly about in Charles's heavy-breathing embrace.

The *kermesse* was subsiding now. Lowing like Mr Potter's cows, and farting at each other in a rather engaging manner, the crowd began to drift away. 'Come on, let's go,' I said crisply to my drunken kamerad. I looked for my policeman, but there was no sign of him anywhere.

Back at the hotel it was clear that Charles was even more drunk than I'd supposed. He put his arm round my neck again when we got in the lift together, and he must have already pressed the Number 4 button, because when the lift stopped he dragged me out to the door of my own room, and I had no choice but to open it with my card.

Once inside he collapsed on the bed, and that was a relief, except that I now began to wonder what to do with him.

The Dutch have two kinds of gin: 'Oude Ginevra' and 'Junke' ditto – something like that. Charles smelt now as if he'd taken a bath in both of them. And on my bed too. I didn't bother shaking him. As I contemplated him it occurred to me to wonder if Cloe was back yet, after tearing off like that with the young Dutch persons, as if on some spree of her own. Wearing my red hat too, although anyone could spot she's not that type at all. A red hat type I mean. Like me.

As Charles remained unconscious on the bed and showed no signs of reviving, I decided I had better check on the Cloe situation. I rummaged in the corpse's pockets – it gives one an odd feeling of power and I rather enjoyed that – and found the plastic card for their room. I went down: no Cloe. So I put a note on the pillow saying Charles was flat out in my room. And she could come and fetch him.

That gave me some satisfaction, but as I went back to the lift it struck me that it would be much more satisfying not to leave a note at all, and to let Cloe wonder where Charles was. That would be my revenge on the tiresome girl. She would come up to my room, and there she'd find the beast, and me in bed beside him. I'd get some of his clothes off and shove them under the duvet, and there we'd both be, enjoying a peaceful post-coital slumber.

That's what it would look like any way, and though the truth would no doubt come out later it would give Cloe a nasty turn, and me a most acceptable revenge. So I went back and removed the note.

Positively chuckling over this prospect I reached my room. No sooner had I slipped in when an amorous Charles positively fell on me. He'd recovered enough for that anyway. Indeed he made lumbering efforts to waltz me round, until he nearly fell over a chair. Then he announced the intention of spending the night with me.

That was poetic justice if you like. Of course I had no intention of letting him make love, but I surmised that he was too far gone for that – even with the boy he must now in a bleary way suppose me to be – and that I could still fulfil my scheme without any risk to myself. Did I say I loved Charles, by the way? Well yes, and I still did, or I suppose I did; but I must admit that since meeting my policeman my perspective on that sort of thing had changed somewhat.

In any case there was no point in paying Charles the compliment of rational opposition, as someone says in Jane Austen. I went to the loo, undressed there, and came back still wearing his blue silk dressing gown, the one I'd had on all evening, and that went with the red hat. I found him sitting on the bed with his head in his hands. Clearly he'd been waiting for me to vacate the loo, for he got up in a hurry, rushed in there and was violently sick.

After a long pause he came out wiping his mouth on what I saw was my vest. I ask you! I suppose he thought it was the face towel. He drank the bottle of mineral water and took several deep breaths. Then he advanced on me with deter-

41

mination. I was sitting up in bed by this time, still wearing his dressing gown of course.

I had no trouble. In fact I began to feel quite maternal as I tucked him up. In a few seconds he was asleep and snoring. Not very loud – I will say that for him.

I chuckled again as I lay down beside him. Things seemed to be working out very well, and any second I expected Cloe to come knocking on the door. I decided I would open it with nothing on, just to show her, and that wouldn't have been hard as I'd taken off the dressing gown anyway. I knew I had no more to fear from Charles.

But then another thought struck me, just like a thunderbolt, and I couldn't think why I hadn't thought of it before. Suppose my policeman were to come in for me during the night, in his quiet sure way?

No reason why not. And yet I'd no sooner had the alarm than I had the relief of realising, goodness knows how, that it wouldn't happen. My policeman was a man of mystery, and that was what appealed to me about him: but the great thing about a man of mystery is that he understands the situation. My policeman understood me and my situation through and through – silly as it may sound to say so. He knew when to come and when not to come – I was suddenly sure of that – and what could make for a more satisfactory relationship? I felt I could repose upon him.

With that straight in my mind I had nothing more to do than to lie equally straight on my back, like a crusader's wife, beside the unconscious Charles, and to wait with the keenest expectations and amusement for Cloe to come bounding up to my room.

That being so, the next thing I knew was that the morning light was shining through the curtains. Charles was still asleep. Cloe had not come. I myself must have been more tired than I realised; after the previous night no doubt and the exertions of the *Kermesse*, although my intake of old or young Ginevra there had been a decidedly modest one, at least compared to what must have been heroic potations on the part of Charles, and Cloe.

Life's odd though. Cautiously raising myself on one elbow, with a very definite feeling of disappointment of what had, and had not, happened, I saw Charles all huddled up and vulnerable beside me, and realised that I did love him rather a lot, in a way. If Cloe had come in at that moment to reclaim him I would have said so. I might even have told her to get lost because he seemed to be mine now. More definitely, if he had woken up and been amorous at all, I should have been happy to oblige him.

But alas no. Life's not like that; nothing of the kind occurred. And Cloe still did not come. I got up and had a bath and dressed, and poked Charles once or twice. He groaned. I found some Alka-Seltzers and held him by the hair and forced him to drink them up with some tap water. Finally I pulled him out of bed and he staggered into the bathroom where I heard him retching again. How deeply unattractive men are, when they are; but the same is no doubt even truer of women.

He was dressed at last, and we went down together to their room. Still no Cloe.

What could have happened to her? The bed had not been slept in, and it seemed clear she had not come back to the hotel. Had she got involved in some way with the crowd of young persons she had gone off with? Had she taken drugs and added to the stupor that a tidy drop of gin must anyway have caused? Had she ended up in one of their beds?

There seemed to be no knowing. I cast a covert glance at Charles to see how he was taking the disappearance of his beloved – if she was his beloved. But he was too hungover, I suppose, to do more than pass a hand across his weary brow and hiccup a few times. I decided breakfast would be the best thing for him, and for myself too.

The matter of Cloe could wait. Girls like her have a strong instinct for self-preservation. Whatever she'd been up to, it wouldn't really amount to much. She wouldn't boast about it either, when she condescended to return to us. She would look smiling, in reply to our jokes and our curiosity. Sort of quietly enigmatic.

My hunch was that she'd done no more than be carried off by some young Dutch people she'd met at the dance, and sleep off its effects wherever they lived. Maybe some single little Dutch boy, or girl, had taken a fancy to her. Whatever it had been she would hardly have bothered to ring the hotel. She wouldn't have known the number, and in any case they might all have been too merry to think of it.

So I allowed myself to think, but secretly I had begun to feel rather worried. A worry I was not going to share with Charles, even if he had been in a fit state to take it in. I daresay I wanted to bring him back to life for myself, and make him more aware of me on my own.

If so, no soap. Urged on by me, Charles made some sort of effort to eat his breakfast, but he could only manage coffee and fruit juice. It braced him a bit but in the wrong direction. He withdrew from me and became morose. My own sprightly consumption of cheese and Parma ham and hard-boiled eggs must, it's true, have been nauseating to watch for a man in his state, and I don't blame him for averting his gaze.

Nothing annoys a man more than being looked at lovingly by a woman for whom he feels no desire at the moment. Charles must have desired me in his drunkenness, and I suppose that was something. I had my trousers on of course this morning, but I was still wearing his blue watered silk dressing-gown, and I had pinned on and readjusted the white cravat thing that Cloe had made for me to go with the red hat.

It didn't look so good this morning of course. She had constructed it most ingeniously out of bathroom tissues, and sort of pinned it in ruffles high on my neck, just like in the picture. The critic who wrote the catalogue made a great

44

point of how clever old Vermeer had 'modelled the striking white cravat by stroking away parts of the white paint with a blunt instrument'. That was more or less what Cloe had done with the tissues. A talented girl, Cloe.

But it didn't work this morning. Maybe everyone else was feeling a bit hungover too. I intercepted one or two glances from our fellow-guests, but they weren't full of admiration and amusement as they had been last night. Perhaps because I had no red hat on, but in any case the party was all too clearly over. Truth to tell, some of the other breakfasters looked as if they might have been on the marijuana the previous night, or even the cocaine or the Ecstasy. I believe the Hague is a lot more straitlaced than Amsterdam, and our hotel seemed very respectable, but it obviously had a cosmopolitan clientele.

Could Cloe indeed have been introduced to some drugs last night? Was she sleeping off the effects somewhere? Or could they have been more serious? Could she have been taken to hospital?

No, Cloe was much too fond of herself to do anything like that. Even after the old or the young Ginevra, of which she had certainly freely partaken.

The funny thing about being a threesome, when you get used to it, and even if you are a bit in love with one of the others, is that any two of you begin to feel quite lost in the absence of the third. That was happening to me now, and no doubt it was happening to Charles too. He was making a pretence of reading the Dutch newspaper, and he often put a hand to his head, which must have been splitting. We had nothing to say to one another.

It was now nearly eleven o'clock, and quite clear that we were both beginning to feel a bit worried. If Cloe had sneaked in while we were having breakfast we should have seen her; and she was not at all the sort of girl who would have sneaked in, in any case. She would have come tripping up to our table and sat down with a self-satisfied smile.

So had she been raped and thrown in a canal? Strangled? Her throat cut? I could feel we were both beginning to think things like that. Yet somehow one can't feel it's what happens in Holland, only back in Dickensian old England. Neither of us mentioned it, but by now we had taken to going every few minutes to the reception desk, to see if any message had been left. Or a policeman waiting to break us the news, I thought to myself apprehensively. Then I thought, a policeman – my God! – suppose it were my policeman! I knew it couldn't be somehow – he couldn't be that sort of policeman, although after all, why not?

Twelve o'clock came, and still no Cloe. No message in the ever polite but by now slightly bored reception area. No call received. We discussed going out and looking for her in the streets. But what would be the point of that? We couldn't both go, in case she came back and found no one here. And although neither of us said so, I think both of us were reluctant to do anything without the other. We wanted to cling together. There was nothing tender about this on my side, and it gave me no satisfaction now to be alone with Charles. But I didn't want to be left on my own, still less to wander purposelessly abut the streets without him.

Charles looked increasingly helpless, and the glances he directed at me more and more dependent. That did not please me either. But it was clear I must do something. What would the girl in the red hat have done?

The art experts would say don't be stupid: she can do nothing because she has no past and no future, no cares and no worries, no tiresome acquaintance, no love troubles. She is just paint, beautiful paint. She is so real, so alive in herself, that she has left all the contingencies of living behind. That is why the admiring crowds in the gallery gather around her and worship in silence.

Well, they can keep all that. I am, have been, a girl in a red hat, and I can tell you it isn't like that at all. On the contrary. The main thing is that you don't know what is going to happen from one moment to the next. Stimulating? Jolly exciting, what? Well, yes and no. But that is what it feels like.

So I rang the police. Or rather I got the hotel to do it for me. The reception man rather enjoyed the idea, you could see that. And he had quite a long chat, in Dutch naturally, with whoever it was at the other end.

Within ten minutes a police person had arrived. I say 'police person' because she was a woman. That was disappointing, and I don't mind saying so. She was a nice little thing, however, in a uniform of rich grey-blue, rather Vermeeresque. She didn't waste time asking questions, but suggested we should accompany her to the 'installation' as she called it, which was presumably the police station.

I liked walking with her through the streets and past the canals, with Charles trailing a bit behind. She chatted away in good English about what we had seen and done in the Hague, and how we liked Holland, and all that. I suppose all police persons are told to be nice nowadays, but I felt she was nicer than they would have been at home. Pure prejudice no doubt.

And certainly this pleasantness was dashed when we arrived. I expect all such offices are the same. It was full of drivers quarrelling, and there was a sickly and disagreeable smell of marijuana, though whether it was being smoked by the police or had been confiscated from the bad guys one naturally couldn't tell. Our policewoman asked us to wait a few moments in the reception area. Rather surprisingly for clean little Holland the wooden chairs had a worn and greasy look. I kept wondering whether my own policeman could be here, and half hoping, half dreading that he might come round the door.

But no; it was a blond and smart young man who came for us after a few minutes out of an inner office. He ushered us in and sat us down. What could he do for us?

I started to explain, Charles remaining more or less mute. The policeman nodded intelligently. So we had been at the

47

Vermeer dance celebration, as he believed they had called it. He had heard it was best fun – he wouldn't have minded being there himself – and he produced, as if in conformity with the police training manual, a terrifically human smile. And had we been dressed up a bit, as the organisers had suggested? Yes; my friends had been the cavalier and the girl with the wineglass, and I had gone as the girl in the red hat.

At the mention of the red hat the policeman suddenly seemed to remember something. Excusing himself he went out for a moment. Charles and I looked at each other, each aware that the other was being careful to look expressionless.

The young policeman came back again, carrying a large ledger. He put it down carefully, explaining it was the log book of the night officer. In accordance with standing orders no doubt, he and his colleagues on day shift had taken a look at it this morning. It had come round to him not long before we came in, and when I mentioned the red hat, he'd recalled an item entered at seven that morning.

That was bright of him, because it said nothing about a hat. It seemed that a busdriver on his way to work had noticed something in the water as he walked down a canal street not far from the Town Hall. The Dutch are so clean, obsessively so about their canals, that he paid some attention to it. It was half floating and shapeless, definitely red. As the busdriver stopped and peered – here the policeman craned his thick neck forward and gestured with his arms – he had seen what he described as a red cloud spreading away from the object in the water. A red streak was travelling sluggishly some way down the canal.

Perhaps it was part of a body? – perhaps even part of a female body? Blood coming out of it. In his excitement the busdriver had nearly fallen in. The policeman smiled understandingly. The busdriver saw another pedestrian not far off and ran to get hold of him. They examined the thing together for some minutes, and then, being civic-minded and responsible Dutch persons, decided they had better find a police-man.

But when it was finally fished out the object proved to be nothing more than some cloth and feathers, coming to pieces, which must have been recently and crudely dyed because the dye was running out of it into the canal.

'But that's my hat!' I exclaimed, jumping up. 'It must be!'

The policeman looked politely interested. What had happened to the thing found in the water? He really could not say; for after the pair of pedestrians had found it was not part of a corpse, but only some discarded rubbish, they had lost interest and gone off on their own business. The policeman they had summoned had only logged the incident because such was the rule when they were called on for help by any member of the public. As for the object itself, it had no doubt been deposited in a litterbin, somewhere in the vicinity.

'You were wearing it at the dance, the last night?' enquired the policeman in a soothing voice, as if courtesy compelled him to continue to humour these English visitors.

'No – I mean yes – I was wearing it at the dance. But then my friend wore it when she went home,' I told him, passing over the circumstances in which I and Cloe had exchanged hats. 'We got separated, you see, and we went back to the hotel, and she still hasn't come back.'

I paused, aware that this sounded pretty feeble, and mute Charles at my side was giving me no help at all.

But if he thought it feeble and frivolous the policeman was too polite to say so.

'I understand,' he said solemnly, 'and now you are wishing to find your hat, if that can be done. Perhaps it can.' He consulted the ledger again, and told us the canal, the street, and the nearest street crossing to the point where the hat had been located. Getting out paper and pen he wrote all this down in large round block letters, folded the piece of paper, and handed it to me with a slight flourish.

I longed to say to him: 'But don't you see that our friend

may be at the bottom of the canal, if the hat was found floating in it?' But for some reason I could not bring myself to do so. It would have jarred the decorous atmosphere too much. Here the three of us were, like a Dutch *tronie* picture: gallants conversing with a young officer of the guard – something like that – and there could be no upsetting the relaxed and formal pattern.

Besides, I didn't really think for a moment that Cloe could be where I had wanted to say she might be. No doubt that was why I hadn't said it. Cloe and her band of strayed revellers must have tossed the hat about – my hat – amid much hearty Dutch laughter, until it had fallen into the canal. Then they had staggered off home. And knowing Cloe as I did I thought it most unlikely she would have ended up in one of their beds. Cloe was a wary girl, even when she'd had a few, however much she liked to show off. At the close of the party she might well have found, or been offered, somewhere to sleep. But for her there would have been no strings attached.

So I reasoned in my head; and yet I did not entirely believe myself either. This picture of how she had behaved was too plausible for it to correspond with anything that had actually happened. Could she not rather have found herself alone, more or less abandoned, and so tossed Vermeer's hat she'd made for me into the water, in some momentary fit of pique or jealousy? Somehow that seemed to me more likely, but it did not solve the problem of where Cloe was now.

I sat down again with a glance at Charles, who was looking awfully seedy. No wonder he was giving me no help. He has no head for drink, even though he thinks he ought to go too far from time to time. He must still have been feeling terrible.

Now it was the policeman's turn to stand up, as if intimating with his usual politeness that our interview was at an end.

'But please,' I said, trying to be earnest as well as feminine

50

and confiding, 'you will try to find our friend, won't you? We've really no idea where she might have gone, and we *are* beginning to get anxious.'

He waved his big hands in a gesture that was more like a Gallic shrug.

'If your friend should still be missing we shall take measures to find her. Please keep in touch with me.' And he gave me a card, like a salesman. Showing us to the door, he added with a smile of reassurance, 'We are only young once, as I am sure she know.'

I was rather relieved to find that his English was not quite perfect. It made him seem more likely to be good at his job.

I noticed he had extremely blond eyelashes. A lot of Dutchmen seemed to have them.

Should we first follow the policeman's directions and try to retrieve the red hat? I wanted to, mostly out of curiosity to see where it had been found, but I could feel that Charles was impatient now to get back to the hotel, and of course his feelings did him credit.

As I hurried him along, still giving an occasional groan, I kept thinking, naturally enough I suppose, of what could have happened to Cloe, who seemed more present in her absence than she would have been in the flesh. It is odd to think what people one knows well are doing when they're not there. It's like pictures one knows well, and of course I thought of the Vermeers, and the girl with the pearl earring, and what things she got up to outside the picture. What things did I get up to, if it came to that? And I thought of my policeman, and our night in bed together. He was an odd person, but lovable surely? At least I had found him lovable.

Absent heads, though, must be odder even than absent bodies. What did Cloe really want, secretly think about, lust after? I had no idea, and nor, I imagine, had Charles. But could her disappearance have anything to do with it, whatever it was? Something must have happened to her – I was beginning to know that inside myself – but I was not prepared to think about what sort of thing it might be. Surely the sort of things that might happen to a girl in England wouldn't happen here? And yet why not? They could happen anywhere. Nothing more certain than that.

I began to feel that a great deal could depend on whether Cloe had stayed with the band of party-goers – party-leavers rather – or whether she had gone off on her own, perhaps to walk back alone to the hotel.

By this time we were back at the hotel ourselves. And, well, you've guessed it – still no Cloe.

Charles hung miserably round the reception area while I pursued the enquiries. Were they *quite* sure nothing had been heard, no phone message come in? Could there have been any misunderstanding about whom we were trying to find? The hotel was as polite as ever and as baffled as we were, although they seemed baffled more by the persistence of our enquiries than by the question of what we were enquiring about.

I had slipped naturally into the role now of taking a firm line with Charles. Up in their empty room I told him to get his head down and try to sleep off his hangover. He seemed eventually to welcome the suggestion, and I got him into bed. I hung the *Do Not Disturb* sign on the door. If Cloe came back she would pay no attention to it anyway.

As soon as I unlocked the door of my own room with the plastic card I knew there was someone in there. It couldn't be the maid or she would have left the door open. Oh no, it was my own policeman, lying on the bed. All six foot four of him, or however much it was. As I stood staring down at him it looked like even more than that.

As soon as he saw me he got up, opened the door, and hung that *Do Not Disturb* sign on the handle. He should have done that sooner, to be sure of the maid not coming in, or perhaps he wouldn't have minded her coming in, so that he could have a go at her too?

This flippant yet unjealous thought passed through my

mind, I own. Whatever I felt about him, I did not feel possessive, and the chambermaid, an Indonesian girl, was a good looker. But I watched him with mixed feelings as he put out the sign and closed the door again. Whatever I felt about him seemed irrelevant to the present crisis, and to the disappearance of Cloe, which began to show every sign of becoming not only a mystery but a serious matter.

His expression, as I contemplated him, was grave and amiable. No means of telling what he had in mind. He stood in the middle of the room, with his hands on his hips, and looked down thoughtfully at me. I had forgotten what he was wearing in the lift but it was probably the same suit, neat dark and massive, that he now had on. It went with his dark complexion and his big handsome nose. His shirt was a subdued white and his tie almost black. Very much in the continental manner.

Our last encounter had not been of the visual sort exactly – more tactile. And as he stood there I found myself wondering what he would look like now with nothing on, in the way that men are said to do with women. It reminded me of my little fantasy in the Mauritshuis, about all of us being naked like a Last Judgement, and yet ignoring each other in our worship of Vermeer's pictures.

I half expected him to pull me on to the bed, or to straddle me on his knee as he had done previously in the lift. I wouldn't have resisted, but I would rather that it did not happen. Nor did it. It seemed that he had more important matters on his mind. And what he turned out to have on his mind was Cloe, and what had happened to her.

Perhaps that was not so surprising after all. He was a policeman, or at least he had told me he was, and he might have been operating in partnership with his colleague back at the police 'installation'. But somehow I knew already, and as if by instinct, that wasn't the case: and it turned out that I was right. I asked him straightaway if he had consulted with his colleagues down at the 'installation', and if he knew anything about what had happened to Cloe.

He looked embarrassed. Even that look suited those big dark features of his, which I was beginning to get so fond of.

'I'm not quite that kind of policeman,' he said.

Well then what kind was he? I asked him.

'Israeli police,' he said. '*Mossad*.' Had I heard of it?

Well, I mean, who hasn't heard about *Mossad*. I goggled at him.

'I don't believe you,' I said. And I expect I giggled a certain amount. It does come over me at moments of surprise sometimes.

No one less giggly than my policeman could well be imagined. He looked grave, very grave indeed, which of course suited him more than ever. He didn't bother to reply to what I had said, and it had been pert of me, I admit.

What he wanted to talk about was Cloe. He knew where she was. He knew what had happened to her. And that she was in danger.

For a moment I felt, you know, genuinely panicked. And sick: as you do when you hear on the news that a girl has disappeared, and there doesn't seem much doubt about what's happened to her. But something in the very gravity of my policeman reassured me; as if, since he looked like that, it could not be quite so bad after all.

'She's not dead?' I babbled. 'Not in a canal? With her throat cut, or strangled? You're not breaking it to me gradually, are you?'

It appeared that he wasn't. And then an extraordinary story began to come out. I mean he began to tell me what had happened. Or so he said.

He didn't look at me directly while he spoke. And he still seemed apologetic, as if regretting the necessity of explaining the whole thing to me. It made me feel rather delinquent, for some odd reason, as if he were a doctor with the task of telling me I had got something nasty – Aids or something.

54

Or perhaps a love-child. My fault, but he wasn't going to say so.

As if almost in the same spirit I found myself averting my own head. Withdrawing into my shame, so to speak, for things like that once used to be a cause for shame, apparently. In the same spirit of evasion I opened my bag, as if to fiddle with a comb or compact; and there was the ticket to the Mauritshuis, with the girl in the red hat on it.

I gazed at the picture while he started talking, for it looked as if all this trouble had come on account of the red hat Cloe had made me. And there she was in the picture, whether boy or girl, man or woman. A faintly bluish look round the chin, perhaps just the violet shadow from the extravagant hat brim, under which her bright eyes were looking at me.

It's the picture of Vermeer, perhaps the only one, which has a future, if you see what I mean. That girl or boy is going somewhere, though he or she doesn't know where. None of the others are: they have become their pictures. That red hat person is getting out – is on the way out as she looks at you.

Pretending to fumble inside my bag, I went on looking furtively at the picture while my policeman was talking. I felt hypnotised too by his soft full foreign voice, which I'd never heard so much in action before. Now there seemed no stopping it. And what he was saying seemed enough to make any red hat person's future seem a pretty dicey business. Nicer to stay in Vermeer's other world, where nothing ever changes? But persons with red hats must be prepared not to do that.

He began, strangely enough, by actually *apologising*. For his conduct in the lift, and then for coming into my room like that during the night. I was deeply touched, but also I wanted to burst out laughing. In the end I told him for heaven's sake, it had been a compliment. Which of course I felt it had been.

He explained then that when he was on a case he often got very wrought up, and needed someone for sex pretty urgently. 'Someone?' I asked, feeling, I must admit, rather deflated. 'Well, someone like yourself, if I could make choose,' he said. That mollified me a bit.

But it didn't explain anything, except perhaps that he might be having me on, for sex reasons. Was he really still hoping to do the thing I wouldn't let him do the other night?

But after those preliminaries he really had my attention, so that I soon stopped wondering whether he was having me on or not. In fact I became totally gripped.

He told me that there was a Palestinian terrorist cell operating at this moment in the Hague. A Palestinian diplomat was coming next week for a conference. They planned to assassinate him.

Their cover was a small restaurant. It was called an Israeli restaurant, but in fact it was run by Palestinians. And they made a kind of safe house for the terrorists.

When he told me this I could contain myself no longer. 'But I know this place,' I burst out. 'We went there for supper the other evening.'

And then I thought of the moment I had gone into what I thought was the Ladies, and seen the man with the very white face and little black moustache. The man I was sure I had seen before somewhere, and then remembered the photo from the newspaper. In the most alarming but exciting way what my policeman was telling me fitted in with the man I had seen, who I now felt quite sure must be the chief specialist in whatever terrorist act was about to be carried out.

When I had identified the man I had seen in the restaurant with the photo I had seen in the paper I had regarded it merely as an interesting coincidence. But of course it was much more than that. That man was here for a purpose, and for an obviously wicked one, and my policeman was here to prevent it if possible. He was working undercover for *Mossad*; and suddenly that meant that I too was involved, that I must already be practically working with him on the same secret assignment.

All this was quite abruptly so thrilling, even if it was disconcerting as well, that it almost drove out of my head the question of what had happened to Cloe.

It was my policeman who brought her back, so to speak. He informed me, as if it was the most natural thing in the world, that these Palestinian terrorists had kidnapped Cloe. That did stagger me. In fact it staggered me more than it alarmed me. Why should anyone bother with Cloe? Not that I felt jealous exactly, but it seemed so irrelevant. My policeman and his extraordinary story was my own concern, and it was annoying that Cloe too should turn out to be involved.

Does that sound callous? If so I'm afraid I can't help it. To do myself justice, I felt relieved that one of the more normal newspaper horrors had not overtaken Cloe. She wasn't in the canal. Children playing on the beach at Scheveningen were not going to find a partially decayed arm sticking out of a sand-dune. I know it's irrational, but what had actually happened to her seemed as it were safer, because more fantastic. Not quite believable.

And yet my policeman was making me believe it, whether true or not. It didn't seem to occur to him that I might doubt what he was telling me.

Nor did I. He had a sort of weary professional air now, as if the whole business bored him. It was his *métier*. He would rather be a footballer, no doubt, or design stage-sets, but since he was working for *Mossad* he had no choice but to get on with the job.

His job at the moment was a difficult one. In fact, as I could easily see, it must be quite nerve-racking.

Did the restaurant people trust him, think of him as one of themselves? Up to a point no doubt they did, for his cover had been elaborately arranged. He was their outside man, and he never himself appeared at the restaurant, or conferred with the leader of the terrorist cell, or with any of his associates. He had been truly dismayed to find out what had happened to Cloe.

Was she in danger? I inquired breathlessly. How on earth had it happened? And why?

His big dark eyes up till now had been friendly and relaxed, even bored, but they looked at me sharply when I said that.

He then made it clear that Cloe's abduction was in a sense my own fault, even though I could hardly be blamed for it. Had I not seen the chef when we went there to have supper, and I accidentally opened the door at the back?

I was puzzled for a moment. The chef? One imagined an amiable fellow in a tall white hat and checked trousers, very different from my sinister figure with the white face and moustache. But then I realised my policeman must mean 'chef' in the continental sense of 'chief'.

That was it; and I had seen the chief in his office. For what in retrospect seemed a very long second our eyes had met. I had stared at him, even at that moment beginning to wonder where I had seen him before; and because I was staring at him he seemed to have no choice but to stare back.

That was what did it. Sensitised by those pictures of himself that had appeared in the papers, he must be equally sensitive to the fact that those who saw him recognised him, even if the fact did not necessarily register with them at the time.

Perhaps too a crack terrorist, a thoroughly experienced expert like that, might know by a kind of instant sixth sense that I'd realised who he was. And that I might talk about it, try to find out more, even tell the police.

He would have been quite wrong of course. I should have done nothing, just as I had in fact done nothing, since that first moment in the restaurant. But how was the chief, or chef, to be sure of that?

What a bore for them! And a possible threat too, considering they were planning this murder. Always assuming they really were planning it.

In any case, said my policeman (I couldn't ask *him* whether they really were planning the murder) they decided not to take the risk. They had us watched next day, and at the Town Hall during the dance. And there I was of course, wearing the red hat.

Except that afterwards, when the snatch was planned to take place, it was not me who was wearing it, but Cloe.

My policeman had been wandering ponderously around the room, telling me this in fits and starts. Perhaps his manner was a bit solemn because of the responsibility of telling me all these secrets. Now and then he took a deep breath and passed a hand over his thick mop of dark hair. I felt that he was putting his life in my hands, and Cloe's too of course. I felt he knew he could rely on me absolutely.

More important, I felt I was one of the boys. Or rather that I was the boy himself. He was the man who turned to me in this crisis. And I was naturally the wife too, whom the man turned to for moments of relaxation and repose.

All this under a red hat!

I felt very pleased with myself. Also immensely flattered.

I used to be very fond of fairy stories when I was a 'little girl', although I'm glad to say I never felt in the least like a little girl; and in almost all of them a beautiful maiden is in the power of some witch or wizard, and has to be rescued by some young chap who gets given – most unfairly – all sorts of magic properties with which to do the job.

I felt I had such a magic object. It was the red hat; even though it had disappeared, and had probably come to pieces and would land up in the municipal incinerator. Never mind, it had been mine; and Cloe had made it for me, and she had stolen it from me and worn it herself, with dire consequences. And now it was up to me to rescue her.

The psychiatrists have an expression for this sort of thing, I believe: CRS, or childhood regression syndrome. Very common no doubt, although I don't remember having had it before. But no doubt under the influence of my policeman, with whom I seemed to be fairly rapidly falling in love, I certainly had it now.

I'm not quite sure, come to think of it, how the policeman would have fitted into this sort of fairy-tale. Would be a benevolent wizard in disguise? Or the prince himself, who would fall in love with Cloe and marry her? As I naturally had no wish to marry her myself I could hardly quarrel with that, except that I was damned if I would let my policeman have anything to do with her. I don't know how a fairy-story would take care of that problem.

With all this nonsense in my head I was barely attending to what my policeman was telling me. The point he emphasised was that if I were simply to march into the restaurant and ask to see the 'Chef' they would be so taken aback that they would have to change their plans radically. For a start they would have no choice but to let us both go. They had made a mistake. My whole demeanour would make that quite clear. We were not in the least interested or concerned with who they were, or what they might be up to. So far from recognising the man behind the door, with the moustache and the white face, I had merely been annoyed to find it was not the Ladies.

I don't know how all this would have sounded to someone who wasn't falling in love, as I certainly was. To me at that moment it made perfect sense. Why not?

My incomparable policeman lay down again and sighed heavily. His big polished shoes touched me deeply: I could hardly take my eyes off them. I was his *copain*, his boyfriend, his mistress, his fellow-adventurer .... But I think what appealed to me even more was my own vision of myself as the true wearer of the red hat. I would be coming contemptuously to rescue a cowering Cloe, who had snatched the hat off my head and put it on her own, and been snatched herself in consequence. She had presumed to wear the red hat, and had suffered the appropriate fate.

Effortlessly I would obtain her release. A humbly grateful, a still terrified, a subdued and abject Cloe would be borne off by me, back to the hotel. The hapless and helpless damsel would be restored to a grateful Charles. He would be relieved beyond measure by her return; shamingly conscious that he himself had done nothing to rescue her.

Lost in my daydream I was still conscious of my policeman. He had drawn up one leg in its beautifully creased trousering, and removed the sock and shoe. He was now scratching his big toe thoughtfully.

This was irresistible. I was his wife now, and it was something I could do. I sat down on the bed beside him and took his foot in my lap. I moved his hand away and gently scratched the big toe myself.

'Is the nail bothering you?' I asked him. 'I've got some scissors if it is.'

No, he said, he wanted to make love to me now. Always the same when he was on a job. Nervousness probably. He smiled his big dark smile.

This time I let him do what he had wanted to do the last time, in the night. I could be a boy after all. And since I really loved him.

As we were getting up he produced from his jacket pocket a small glittering complex-looking object, not like anything I had seen before. He did something with it, and there came out of it a hum of static and the sudden remains of a voice. He put it on my chest, and told me to say something, a sentence or two. I said 'I love you', which was all I could think of. He put it to my ear, and I heard my voice (and very silly it sounded I must admit) saying 'I love you'. I believe I may have actually blushed.

He got out a roll of adhesive tape and proceeded to fasten this little thing into my armpit, first wiping me carefully with the end of the sheet to dry off any sweat. I was fascinated by this operation but I couldn't see much of what he was doing because I was sitting on the edge of the bed with my arm stuck obediently up in the air, like a cat's hindleg when it's washing itself. And he was lying on the bed behind me.

'Listen,' he said; and his voice came out of the other little machine asking where I was and what was happening. I said I was sitting in the nude on the edge of my bed in the hotel, waiting for further instructions, and then I burst out laughing. He didn't seem to find it funny at all. He clicked off the little thing in his hand, with a satisfied expression. Then he pulled me over backwards towards him.

He hardly said anything as we got dressed. I had no idea now what time it was. The *Don't Disturb* sign must still be hanging outside the door; and if Charles had come up, which he might well have done, he had obviously respected my sleep, since presumably there was still no news of Cloe. The alternative, which was much more likely, was that he was still asleep himself. Sleeping off that hangover.

The atmosphere had become very fraught. I could feel that my policeman was intensely nervous, and I longed to pat him, kiss him, reassure him as best I could. But another part of me knew that one didn't behave like that in this kind of situation. The odd thing was that I can honestly say I didn't feel nervous for myself at all. I trusted my policeman; and somehow from his manner I felt confident that he had done all the groundwork, so to speak, and had everything under control. His tension, and his silence too, were a reassuring part of all that.

I had my part to play, and I knew it was a kind of stooge part, though quite important to the business of throwing the opposition off balance. I would be a faithful sergeant, or whatever the soldiers are called who are not quite officers. Faithful and responsible in fulfilment of the duty entrusted to me.

I suppose it was love that made my feelings so uplifted. But there it was – they were.

I could feel the hard little knob of the communicator thing in my armpit; and that reassured me. Whatever happened I should be able to speak to my loved one and ask for further instructions. It was part of my equipment, like being a wireless operator; and I even felt the same way about my shoes and trousers as I pulled them on. Back into uniform, as it were.

He was standing up now by the bed, his face expressionless. When I was ready he looked me over, and then nodded almost imperceptibly. It was the sign for me to go. No kisses of course, or anything of that sort. Without another look at him I opened the door and slipped out. I too had become a *Mossad* agent – a junior one, of course.

I had no trouble finding my was back to the Israeli restaurant. It took me about twenty minutes. I once took a wrong turning, probably out of sheer nerves, as I have a good sense of direction and remembered the way perfectly well. There was the usual canal beside the street. It could have been the same one in which the red hat was found, in the vicinity of which Cloe had presumably been made away with.

Somehow I still couldn't quite believe it. I believed my policeman absolutely; but that was because I was in love with him. As a question of belief, and of what had happened to her, Cloe seemed separate. My feelings about her were, after all, distinctly negative. Had they hurt her, even raped her? Had she been tied to a chair, bound and gagged, like the heroine in an old film? Or would she just be sitting in the back of the place somewhere, under the eye of the surly dark-haired young woman who had brought our food – and pretty awful it had been – the other night?

It seemed a hell of a long time ago.

I was frightened myself now, I own: in fact I was trembling. And I didn't like to think of Cloe trembling too, much more violently no doubt, as she sat miserably wondering what they were going to do with her.

If she was there at all. But if she wasn't there, where was she?

Of course I still didn't entirely believe in all this. Indeed it would be truer in a sense to say that I didn't believe in it at all. If I had I would never have gone back, as I was apparently now doing, to the restaurant. But I was in love – I was quite sure of that now – and my lover had just made love to me and sent me off on this thrilling assignment. It was like watching a James Bond film, where you know no one's going to get hurt in the end. Except the villains of course; and even they will just get up and smile and walk away when it's over.

That was the effect my policeman had on me. Because I was in love with him I was playing his game. Whatever it was, Cloe must come into it somehow. And Cloe at least was genuinely not there. Not back with us at the hotel I mean.

That was the fact, when I thought about it, which was definitely disquieting. The rest might be all moonshine. My sweet policeman might be bamboozling me; but when one is in love like that one actually enjoys being bamboozled. And even my policeman couldn't bamboozle Cloe into disappearing. *Something* must have happened to her.

That was the thought which had made my inside begin to churn a bit as I walked across the Queen's Square. I think it's called that, this wide and rather handsome space opposite our hotel. I found myself walking more slowly than I had intended. By the time I reached the Israeli restaurant I was positively dawdling. I'd taken, as I said, a wrong turn once, either out of sheer nerves or from an unconscious wish to get back to the safety of the hotel.

But I remembered what my lover seemed to expect of me. And I could feel the reassuring presence of his little wireless contraption, snug in my armpit. I knew it worked, and that

64

I could call him up on it, like with a mobile phone. Hadn't I said 'I love you' into it?

So when I got there I didn't hesitate. I took a deep breath, opened the door of the little restaurant and marched in.

But I intended to be crafty. I wasn't going to march straight in through the door at the back, confront the little man with the dark moustache, and demand Cloe. For one thing the man might not be there. I would sit down, have a coffee, and sort of get used to the place. Before attempting anything else.

The fact was I felt too nervous to attempt anything else for the moment.

All those little Hague places have the same sort of layout. A longish counter for drinks and coffee drinking, which the Dutch are mad about. And a rather cramped area of small tables. There was no one behind the bar, but the dark girl was sitting reading a newspaper on one of the customers' stools. Otherwise the place was empty.

Just seeing the girl again gave me a turn, though she took no notice of me. I sat down at one of the little tables, near the door, and lit a cigarette. I noticed my hands actually were trembling, like in a film close-up.

After a minute or so the girl looked up and saw me. She got reluctantly off her stool and slouched across. I noticed her black eyebrows were positively matted, and I wondered what she'd be like under the arms and in other places. Foreign girls never shaved, or so I'd heard. Neither did I come to that, but then I didn't need to. And I'd never had a faintly blue chin, like the boy-girl's, under his or her red hat.

It showed how nervous I was, looking at her. All these irrelevant thoughts.

'A black coffee, please,' I said.

I'd lost count of the time. A couple with a child came in and sat down at one of the little tables, where the three of them looked as if they might be waiting to be painted by

Metsu or Pieter de Hooch. Except that they looked like Israelis. Or Palestinians.

Panic was mounting in me. Could Cloe really be here? Could she already be dead? Would I soon be dead myself if I stayed here, and didn't flee precipitately out of the door while there was still time?

I sat and waited for my coffee. Of course it was too absurd to feel frightened. The place was just an ordinary harmless café. Cloe had probably come home by now. Did I really think that? Or did I believe what my policeman had told me?

The coffee came and was awful, which is most unusual in Holland, at least in my short experience. The de Hooch oriental family went away, after exchanging a few laconic indifferent words with the bar-girl. Then she got off her stool and went out at the back. I was left alone in the café.

What was I to do now? As there was no one there I couldn't even pay for the coffee. I could hear voices somewhere at the back, and again I had this vision of Cloe somewhere out there, and it sent a shiver through me, even though I couldn't believe it. How was one to believe such a thing in a place like this, dreary as it was. And yet too, it *was* sinister, just in itself: if only because of the absence of any clientele, or even of piped music. It was a pointless place which must, I was sure, be intended for some quite other purpose – perhaps a safe house for conspirators, perhaps a staging post on the white slave trade? Was that what they were going to do with Cloe?

Why didn't I pull myself together, scoot straight out of the café and off to the police station? – if I could find it again. But I could always ask, and the Dutch were so helpful. Find my blonde police officer, and tell what seemed to be going on? Why didn't I? And my whole body gave a twitch, as if it was trying to force me to get up and make a dash for it.

But no, I was a *Mossad* agent. This place was a hotbed of Palestinian terrorism. I must be loyal to my own policeman and do what he had told me to do; and besides, there was Cloe to think of, if she were really here and in danger.

So I stayed where I was, stuck to my chair, and simply waited. I imagined myself going round to the other side of the bar, if a customer should come in, and doing my best to serve him. I seemed to have become a fixture of the place, at once accepted and disregarded.

And then something did happen at last. The street door opened, and the tall bronzed rather goodlooking man who had been in the bar when we had dinner, came striding in. He paid me no attention, and yet I had the nasty feeling as he walked past that he'd been summoned in some way, instructed – perhaps by the girl – to go round and come in at the door, so as to take a good look at me. See there was no mistake.

I nerved myself. Whether he'd had a good look or not, he hadn't paused; and now I took a breath and said sharply to his back view: 'I'd like to pay for my coffee.'

He stopped and turned round. There was a puzzled look on his handsome face – but was it assumed? – and he said 'Please?' The thing foreigners say when they mean 'What the hell are you talking about?' And yet it didn't seem to me that look of puzzlement was entirely convincing.

I had money in my hand, which I held out, but instead of taking it the irritating fellow pointed towards the back of the café and said 'Please' again. 'Pay,' I said loudly. 'You want toilet?' he replied.

I gave up. I felt extremely reluctant to leave the entrance and go down into the dark jaws of the café; but if I was going to find Cloe I would have to: and besides, there was always the chance that this young Palestinian, or whatever he was, had really failed to understand me, and was as honestly clueless as the whole place appeared to be, however slovenly and surly. I know it sounds naive, but what has to be called my mind was still divided between the two possibilities, just as the face under the red hat is divided between being a boy and being a girl. Was it a café, the little Israeli restaurant that it called itself, or was it something much more sinister? A place where conspiracies and murders could be planned. A place where someone like Cloe might be held a prisoner.

I remembered the drunken Charles at the party, telling me as I pushed him round the dancefloor that I looked like the duck/rabbit syndrome. He'd explained about Freud or somebody, and the image that looked like a duck one way and a rabbit the other, depending on the viewer, and, presumably, on his state of mind.

I thought of all that on the way between my little table and the back of the café: and then there I was again, outside that door with the masculine logo on it. Next to it was the mock Ladies, which I now saw had a ghostly PRI on it, ending in a smear: the door I had gone through when I disturbed the terrorist man with the white face and the black moustache.

As I stopped, and wondered what to do, I was suddenly aware of a firm but gentle pressure from behind. I wasn't being seized or pinched or jostled, it was not even a push. Just that as if in the lift on the Underground one was being impelled from behind by an impersonal crowd thinking only of getting out and getting away.

The pressure increased. In response to it I found myself travelling down a short passage and through a door. The pressure had increased to the point where my legs had to move fast to keep me from falling flat on my face.

But I was through a doorway, and a door shut behind me with a decisive thud.

No doubt it had been done by the handsome bronzed young man. He had conveyed me down a passageway, through a door, and shut me in. I felt stupefied, but still in some odd way, because the whole process had been so gentle I suppose, neither shocked nor unduly alarmed.

The room I was in was dark. Quite dark, but not so much that I couldn't see the outlines of a window, and lights beyond it.

All I could think of for the moment was how ridiculous I must have looked, being quietly shoved along the passage, with my legs trotting along helplessly beneath me. It must have been this feeling of having been made fun of that filled me with sudden fury – well, violent indignation at least, which comes to much the same thing.

Turning round I banged vigorously on the door with both fists, shouting 'Open the door, damn you!' I was surprised at what I was saying; but it did sound the sort of thing a clean-cut Englishman of the old school might say when insulted or attacked by foreigners; and that was what was happening to me, after all.

But nothing more happened; and after I had banged on the door for what seemed quite a time it occurred to me to feel for the handle. I did that, found and turned it, and the door promptly opened. That came as a surprise. I pushed it fully open, and there in the lighted passageway stood the bronzed young man, with his hands on his hips. He smiled a nasty sort of smile at me. Still, a smile it was; and I smiled back, rather ridiculously I admit, as if we were having a game.

'Look here,' I began, 'What do you think you're doing?' I was going on to say that this was no way to behave, when he lowered his head, and the top half of his body too, as if in shame or repentance.

The next moment I was lying doubled up on the floor. How I got there I wasn't at the time in any state to know, but it seems he must have butted me in the stomach with the top of his head.

With my last breath, as it seemed, I let out a great groan or whoop: and then I knew I'd never draw breath again. I was dying.

I was curled up on the floor. My eyes had popped open like a doll's and felt as if they would never close again. I could see at its own level how dirty the oilcloth on the floor was. Very unDutch.

69

My eyes rolled up, and I could see the man who had hit me up above. Perhaps he was going to kick me now, put a boot into me. I couldn't move, but as I was dying anyway it didn't matter.

I couldn't get my breath. Then I could, and it was worse. I was going to live, and as I came back to life I was frightened. Really frightened, for the first time. This was not like being a member of *Mossad*, the trusted assistant of my dear policeman. Nor like being a boy or a girl who is wearing a red hat. This was just awful.

But perhaps if you wore a red hat, and looked like the picture did, this was what happened to you in the end.

I had stopped thinking about Cloe. I was thinking only about myself, and what they were going to do to me. But I wasn't really thinking at all.

I just wanted to lie still, curled up on the floor, and never be noticed again. It seemed to be getting darker. When I tried to move at last my middle hurt so much I almost cried out. But I didn't: I was too much afraid of what might happen if I made a noise.

In fact I must have produced a few suffocated groans as I was trying to get my breath back, but I stopped as soon as I became aware of them. I must have lain on the floor there for some time. Once I thought I heard voices, and I sort of cringed in myself, but no one came and nothing happened. I suppose the bastard who slugged me with his head knew what the effect would be. He'd probably taken some special combat course, and passed out top no doubt. Deservedly. They knew they wouldn't have to bother about me for a long time.

Eventually they would come and pick up the pieces. And what would they do with them? I could guess now. I had only seen the two men, but there might be others. I wondered if they would all be there doing it together.

Somehow I knew – don't ask me how – that they had not done it to Cloe. Even if she were, or had been, here, and in the position in which I seemed to be, she would somehow have got out of the probable consequences. They wouldn't have raped her, I mean. I didn't resent Cloe at that moment for what I felt to be her comparative inviolability; but I knew, too, that it wouldn't apply to me.

It's funny, that sort of thing. Quite why Cloe, who is far more female than me, should be able to charm herself out of that sort of jam I just don't know. Just by being so feminine perhaps, in the oldfashioned sense? Makes them feel protective, or at least sort of deferential. I wonder sometimes if there wouldn't be so many cases nowadays of girls being raped and/or strangled if they behaved in a more feminine way in the first place. A bit paradoxical, but there might be something in that. Wasn't it wanting to get in there like the boys that made them, so to speak, fair game?

Anyway I had been fair game. That seemed clear. And it was entirely my own fault.

I may have been thinking all this later, but I certainly wasn't doing so at the time. I'd other things to worry about. My stomach hurt so much I thought that bastard might have broken something, but there was nothing I could do about it. I got to my knees, all crouched up, and trying to hold on to the wall I managed to pull myself to my feet. The door, in the gloom, was just beside me, and eventually I found the handle. Very very carefully, and quietly, I turned it; I was determined to make no more noise than a mouse.

It was locked anyway; or at least it wouldn't open. I hadn't heard a key turn, but then down on the floor like that I wouldn't have, would I?

I began to grope my way round the room, and over to the pale square of window. There was nothing in the room, not even a chair. It seemed to be unoccupied, or the people who lived in the house were intending to leave soon.

Just groping about like that was hideously painful, so I squatted down in a womb-like position by the window and tried to think. I remembered my watch and found it was getting on for seven o'clock. Charles should have recovered from his hangover by now and be wondering where I was. All on his own, without his two girls.

What about my policeman? I remembered him quite suddenly. When I did think of him it was to feel that he hadn't really any connection at all with what had just happened to me. And yet of course he had brought it about! By enrolling me as his agent in *Mossad*. And sending me off on my first assignment: to rescue Cloe.

How silly it all sounded now. And how improbable. Ever since that frightful blow in my stomach I saw things, so far as I saw them at all, very differently. I was sick, not only from the effects of the blow, but with fear. I crouched on the floor shaking with terror, too paralysed to think about what had happened, or to do anything about it. What was there to do, in any case, except wait for whatever it was they were going to do to me?

And then I did remember something. In fact it seemed extraordinary that I should ever have forgotten, but the nightmare of recent events had blotted it out I suppose. It was the radio receiver thing in my armpit.

My policeman became suddenly real again! How wonderful it would be to talk to him! To tell him what had happened, pour out to him my present troubles and the disastrous situation I seemed to be in. I suppose one can't really pour out anything much on a two-way radio, but I didn't think of that. I only thought of my beloved policeman, and how he would reassure me, and then come and save me.

My sense of relief, and love too of course, was overwhelming. Disregarding the anguish it caused I pulled up my jersey as quick as I could and began to fumble in the near dark with the sticky tape which held the receiver in place. I had to take my jersey right off before I could get at the tape properly, and that made my stomach swim with pain. But I finally got the tape unstuck.

As soon as I held the little thing in my hand I knew there

was something wrong. Although small the real thing had been quite heavy. This was too light. Much too light. It couldn't be the transistor thing at all?

It wasn't. The little thing my policeman had showed me and had tried out with me, was about the size of a bottlecap. Well, this *was* a bottle cap. No doubt about it. It probably had 'Oude Ginevra', or something written on it. I held the thing to the window but it was much too dark to see.

What was I to do now? I did nothing. I sat meekly on the floor under the window, and waited for them to come and do to me whatever it was they wanted to do. Fortunately I was too dazed and baffled to think much about that. Perhaps they would just leave me locked up in this room until I starved. That too didn't concern me. I could think of nothing but the fact that when my policeman was taping the device under my arm, and I had one arm round his neck and the other stuck up straight in the air, he had somehow substituted this object for the real one.

I knew there had been a real one, for I had heard it crackle and speak – I had said 'I love you' into it. And that was true too. He had been behind me on the bed, and my cheek had been against his head. I couldn't see what he was doing. I had just been comforted and reassured by it. And thrilled and excited too, I suppose.

And my policeman had deceived me. Grossly. Crudely. It seemed as if he had delivered me deliberately into the hands of the people who had got me now. Or could there be some other explanation? If so I couldn't think of one. Nor was I really inclined to try.

I'm afraid at this point I started to shed tears. Girls, or boys, in red hats shouldn't do that. I could hear myself making hiccups, honking noises, and agonising it was too, because of the soreness in my midriff. The noises I made were very subdued; I was frightened they might be heard. And ashamed too, I do think. So I sat there with my poor stomach heaving and tears running down my face. Very sorry for myself indeed.

I don't know how long that went on. Probably not so very long actually. I do remember that it soon occurred to me my policeman might indeed have had a plan, even though he had misled me. He could have simply wanted, as it were, to set the cat among the pigeons. For all I knew my arrival had caused general alarm, even despondency, among the terrorists, or conspirators, or whatever they were. They might even now be planning to abandon their whole project and get out. Leaving me locked up in this room. And in that case my policeman, who would have been prowling about outside, awaiting developments, might eventually burst in and rescue me.

The idea cheered me for a second, but for no more than that. Partly because I suddenly heard distant voices and laughter. Whatever they were doing it didn't sound as if they were in a panic and getting ready to leave. It sounded much more as if they might be laughing in anticipation of having themselves a time with me later on. When they were all closed up, and the men – that little one with the black moustache and the bronzed bastard who had butted me – had the leisure to amuse themselves.

I waited, frozen on the floor, wondering if they were going to come for me now. The laughter and the voices died away again. That was some sort of relief. But it had galvanised me into feeling that I must help myself, if there was any possible way I could do it. I had nothing else. My policeman seemed as much of a toy and a delusion as the thing he had given me, the contraption that had turned out to be nothing but a bottlecap. The only real thing was that he had sent me here: and why had he done that?

I refused to try to think. I got up and tried to look out of the window, which was high and narrow. I was shaking now, partly from cold and from the pain inside me, but chiefly from fear. I was going to have to try to get through that window. There was nothing else for it if I wanted to save myself and get away from these people.

By reaching up as far as I could I managed to push at the bottom fastenings. To my surprise the window opened quite easily; and when I saw the darkness and the lights outside – far down they seemed – I began to wish it hadn't. But although my stomach shrieked with agony I forced myself to give a spring, and seized hold of the windowsill outside. My feet were well off the floor now, and I somehow gritted my teeth and forced myself up till I was lying over the sill on my wretched stomach. My behind must have been sticking out into the room, and it occurred to me that if the bronzed bastard should come in he could beat it black and blue with his great hands as he had already done with his head to my front parts. I wasn't going to think of what he might do after that.

It was a real red hat situation, none the less. And I nerved myself by thinking what my prototype would have done, and that I must be worthy in this situation of her, or him. And I wriggled myself a bit further. With my head hanging over the edge I tried to see how far it was to the ground, but it was too dark to know. Immediately below me there was nothing but blackness.

Cloe could never even have got through the window. It cheered me up slightly just to think of that.

Surely the ground, even though I couldn't see it, must be not very far beneath me? Unless of course the front of the Israeli restaurant was at a different height to the back, which, as I lay looking down, seemed all too possible. But I must risk it. I must somehow reverse myself, hang by my hands, and drop.

I reversed myself. It took an infinity of time, trouble and suffering, but I did it. Picture of a girl reversing herself through a window. Done by one of the lesser Dutch masters. Good for a belly laugh from the burghers who had it shown off to them by proud owner. (Vermeer, I knew, had been a

75

picture dealer as well as an artist, and it might just have passed through his hands. I wonder what he would have thought of it.)

I wondered all the more feverishly because of the terror I was in. As I lay draped over the sill, with my legs now dangling outside, I knew perfectly well that I wasn't going to let myself go and fall. I simply couldn't. The idea of doing so was just part of the general nightmare. In reality I was going to do nothing, even if it meant lying there draped over the windowsill all night.

Events took charge, however. A window opened above my head, and I heard voices which sounded horribly close. Someone looking out of the window must surely see me. Even so I could not have moved, I think, but at the next moment something soft and wet flopped against me. Were they torturing Cloe in the room up above by drenching her in cold water, and then stripping her and hanging her clothes out of the window? No, of course not. I realised afterwards that it must have been just a sheet, freshly washed in the thrifty Dutch manner and hung out to drip dry.

But at that moment it unnerved me. I was so startled I must have relaxed the vice-like grip I was keeping on the inside of the sill. I found myself sliding. I tried to grip the sill again, but it was too late. As I slipped I felt wet cloth on my face, seeming to finger for my nose and mouth, and that panicked me still more, so that my own fingers had no chance to hold on to anything. The next second I was falling.

I've no idea how far it was. But I had registered the fact that it was a good way to the ground, and that I should probably be killed or seriously injured, when I found myself under water – ice-cold water.

I was deluged and half drowned by the splash I made, falling in feet first. But when the deluge subsided I found the water was only up to my waist, and under it I was up to the knees in soft mud.

Strangely enough I felt chiefly relieved at having escaped the nightmare embrace of all that soft wet linen, which had enfolded me like a sort of shroud as I lay over my window-sill. Had they known I was there, and been trying to stifle me, as an immediate measure to prevent my escape? Even to my wild ideas of what was going on that seemed rather unlikely.

I don't know how I got out of the water. I couldn't have done it at all if there hadn't been a sort of wooden staging, which I had providentially just missed in my fall. That thick soft mud seemed to have absorbed my arrival almost without noticing it; and it would have happily kept me there for ever if I hadn't forced myself with frantic efforts on to the slimy woodwork, which was less than a foot above the water. Again disregarding the agonised protest of my sore stomach I inched myself like a frog until my legs were clear of mud and water. I suppose the place was a kind of barge harbour, long disused.

I looked up fearfully at the place I must have fallen from. I made out the window, which was still dark. Quite high too – fifteen or twenty feet.

I was so soggy with mud and water I felt I weighed a ton. It was an effort to creep away, but I found a sort of towpath beside a proper canal, though only after I had crawled over a garden fence and got my hands and face well stung by nettles. Once on the towpath I tried to run. My trousers were heavy as lead, but I panted along, wanting only to get as far as I could from that vile restaurant.

At last I came out on a back street, which was at least lit up at intervals. I could hear voices now, and I shrank away. My nerve really had gone. After what had happened I was terrified of being seen by anyone, let alone in the state I was in after scrambling out of the canal. Suppose the people at the restaurant were out looking for me? The thought of the bronzed man turned my poor sore stomach over.

Dripping water I slopped along furtively at the edges of

the street, and when I heard voices behind me I bolted blindly into the dark doorway of a kind of hovel – it seemed a pretty run-down sort of area for the spotless Hague. A young couple came walking hand in hand down the middle of the street. They had heavy shopping bags in their free hands, and looked exactly like my idea of Hansel and Gretel.

I must say the Dutch are sweet. They had gone past and into the dark again before I finally found the courage to make a halloing noise after them. I must have looked a sight when I appeared, but they were so polite and tactful. They overwhelmed me at once with offers of help, and with apologies too – they seemed to think it was their fault I'd fallen into one of their canals.

For that was what I said had happened, of course. How I'd come to do it I didn't specify. People in England might have been sympathetic, but they would have found the situation amusing as well. Thank God the Dutch aren't funny about things like that, if indeed they're funny about anything. But no doubt they have a national sense of humour, just the same as us.

This young couple wanted only to succour and to cherish me. They uttered cries of concern, in fluent English of course. I must come home with them, I must, and take off my wet things. They could find me something to wear. And which place was I staying – with friends? in a hotel? – they would take me back there of course, and see me safe.

They were so sweet that I started to cry. That seemed to them quite natural, and they made cooing noises over me. I'm sure that one would only find such kindness abroad, or even only in Holland. But perhaps if it happened the other way round people would feel the same thing about the English. It's all a matter of perspective probably.

They lived in a little flat, not very far off. They gave me a hot shower; and the girl said she'd wash my things and bring them round to the hotel. Or perhaps I could come and see them again, tomorrow evening, after work, and that would be a great pleasure for them. The atmosphere of caringness and goodness was a bit relieved – and I must say it *was* a relief by that time – by all the fun and giggles when the girl – her name was Hannelore – was helping me on with a cotton skirt of hers, together with a blouse and a vest and pants to go under them. All that part of it did seem to her to be very funny, and I hadn't the heart not to join in. Her husband or boyfriend, I don't know which it was – remained modestly in the living-room while Hannelore was organising me, but he joined in the fun when she led me out to show him. The Dutch can laugh; and now they seemed to find me at once innocent and comic, like a new wooden toy. They gave me coffee and cake, and a glass of old Geneva, in which we drank an unspecified toast. They were quite uncurious about me and where I had come from. They seemed a very self-sufficient couple.

The girl kept patting me to see if I was warm; and they both seemed to want me to stay, so that they could go on laughing kindly at me. But I said I must really be getting back to my friends in the hotel, and they quite understood that. They would show me the way of course. And bring my clothes tomorrow. Naturally I begged the girl not to go to any trouble, but I could positively see her ironing my damp trousers with a far-away look as if in a picture. Girl ironing a pair of trousers. And she would be feeling the material with an interested hand, running her thumbs up and down the discreetly herring-boned tweed cloth ....

On the way back formality, even a certain constraint and shyness, began to grow between us; and presently they were politely asking if I had been to the Vermeer exhibition, and what had I thought of it. Even in the midst of my adventures, and all the absurd and dreadful things that had happened to me, I felt a sort of regret about this, an odd wish to lead the rest of my life, as it were, in the comforting company of just such a sweet young couple as this. But it was no good. I had to go back to the hotel and find out what was going on. And I had no wish whatsoever to do so.

But we were nearly there. The hotel was quite an impressive one, and I think my youthful pair felt suddenly shy when they saw its lights across the Queen's Square. We came to a halt as if by mutual consent, and then awkwardly shook hands.

I felt a strong desire to stay with them, instead of having to go in – back to whatever was going on in the hotel. If only I could have remained in their little flat for days, for weeks and years! Perhaps as their au pair girl when they had a baby, or as a servant who would vacuum the floor, and pour milk from one jug into another?

But that was not the destiny of a girl, or was it a boy, in a red hat. After my recent experiences I saw that all too clearly. I thought I had been playing a sort of game, but it wasn't a game at all. It was going to be my life.

And how much I wished it wasn't, at that moment. I felt so safe with that young couple. The girl had put her arm through mine, as if to support me. A cold fresh wind – the Hague is very near the sea – blew up that unfamiliar skirt I was wearing, so that I shivered. Feeling me do so the girl pressed me to her, as if to soothe a small frightened animal. What a good mother she would soon be making. The thought went through my head as we all three gazed across at the hotel lights: and I knew too that it would never happen to me. A man might butt me in the stomach so that it felt, and no doubt was, black and blue. A man might behave to me in bed as my policeman had done, and then betray me, and I would still love him. That was about it; and that was about all.

The young man was saying to me, 'Your friends will take care of you now.' His girl said nothing, but she squeezed my arm a little. We continued to stand in silence, and again I began to cry.

I stopped almost as soon as I started, for it was not like me at all. Hastily I said it was too kind of them to come tomorrow, but they mustn't, they would be busy, they wouldn't have the time. That seemed to restore things to normal, and the girl said matter-of-factly that she would come in with my clothes when she got home from her office. 'Oh, but you must come in for a drink then,' I said. 'Both of you.' Tomorrow was supposed to be our last day. (I remembered that afterwards – too late – and then I remembered that I hadn't said a word about Cloe's disappearance. Or thought about it. There seemed reasons – good and sufficient ones – why she had gone clean out of my head.)

They murmured something. They had become all shy again; but I think they were pleased to have been invited. An invitation of any sort is probably quite a serious thing in Holland.

I kissed Hannelore on the cheek, in the English fashion. She seemed startled but pleased; and though I saw her boyfriend edge away with a slight look of alarm on his face, I pursued him and kissed him too. If he thought me some unnatural and shameless hermaphrodite that couldn't be helped. Perhaps I was one.

'Your friends will be caring for you,' he said in faintly relieved tones. But already I was walking away across the dark square, and waving back to them. As I went into the hotel I saw them still standing there, looking after me. How much I regretted leaving them, but what else was there to do? The whole day, the whole two days, had been so strange, such a nightmare in a sense: but I felt none the less that I belonged there now – they had revealed themselves as the sort of life I apparently had to lead.

All the same I was unprepared for the sight of Charles and Cloe, sitting peacefully in the dining-room together, eating their dinner.

Of course I went up to them – what else was there to do? – although I honestly think they wouldn't have noticed me if I'd gone past them up the stairs, or turned round again and

81

run out of the hotel. I might have been just in time to catch up with my little Dutch couple. I longed for them at that moment, absurd as such a longing was. For my head seemed full of darkness and despair, and a horrid reluctance to allow myself to think about any of the things that had happened to me lately. I shrank away from them, just as I did now from Cloe and Charles, sitting there in the dining-room.

When had she got back? And how? But I didn't really want to know. I was too absorbed in my own feelings. Dark miserable feelings about my loved one, the policeman, and the shock and humiliation of what had happened to me. That it might have been much worse, and would have been if I hadn't managed to get away, did not occur to me at that moment. I had no cause to congratulate myself on my escape. I was just confused and miserable and brought low.

*

Very low.

All the same I had to go up to Cloe and Charles, sitting at their table in the dining-room. There was no alternative.

They saw me threading my way through the other diners. They had a conscious look at once, though they did not exchange glances.

'So whatever happened to you?' said Cloe brightly, looking up and down at the clothes I was wearing.

'I rather thought it was something that happened to you,' I countered. But I didn't really feel like this kind of thing. Banter between old friends, that is.

Charles went on eating his Dutch apple pie as if whatever was said was no affair of his. And this was the man who had tried to make love to me last night, hadn't he, and accompanied me to the police station this morning, groaning with hangover, to report our worries about an absent Cloe! I noticed he had a piece of Gouda cheese on top of his pie.

'We had better order dinner for you,' said Cloe. 'If it's not too late.' She sounded as if she rather hoped it would be.

'Oh, don't bother about me,' I told her. I glanced all the same at my wristwatch and found it wasn't there. It must have been scraped off somehow, no doubt while I had been climbing out of that window and falling into the canal.

'I don't want anything, thank you,' I said. 'I've had it already,' I added, feeling for the moment that I had, and that it had seriously disagreed with me.

Cloe shrugged. 'You're a lucky girl then. The dinner here is not exciting. We should have gone out. But Charles thought we ought to wait in for you.'

'That was big of him. He didn't seem so keen earlier on to wait in for you.'

It was graceless, not even neat; and Cloe showed her contempt for my remark by ignoring it without the slightest effort. I decided, though rather half-heartedly, to try again. 'You could always have gone out to that Israeli place,' I said.

'Not bloody likely!' exclaimed Cloe, with what seemed a vigorous candour. From the way she behaved I couldn't tell what sort of act she was putting on, let alone why. Like a lot of girls Cloe likes to act as though fascinating things were always happening to her: but tonight she seemed to be holding it calmly in, as if something so exciting might really have happened that she wasn't going to talk about it, at least not to me.

Well, if she was going to be clear, vigorous and candid, I decided to be the same, in spades. I would expose myself; I would drop any possible guard.

'All I managed to do,' I said, 'was fall into a canal.'

They laughed at me together then, as intended. And they looked relieved as well. As if my coming clean about such a comic humiliation made it easier for them to say nothing about what they had been doing, particularly Cloe.

I said I had gone out again to look for Cloe while Charles was sleeping off his hangover (I felt I owed him the dig, and he looked as if he acknowledged it). My idea, I said, had been to find the canal in which the red hat had been seen. Quite irrational, I agreed, looking closely at Cloe, but there just might have been some further clue there as to what had happened to her.

A Dutch couple had pulled me out, I told them.

The ball was now in Cloe's court. Indeed it was on the tip of my tongue to demand bluntly what had happened to her; but I realised it would be wiser to appear incurious. Let her think the advantage was all on her side.

So I went on brightly telling them my own banal adventures, and how this sweet young Dutch couple had helped me out of the canal. I amused them by showing off the ratty little cotton skirt, patterned in a Mondrian print, like the crocuses, which the girl had apologetically lent me. I felt a traitor as I did so. I felt I hated Cloe and Charles: I wished I had said nothing at all to them of the Dutch girl and boy: I experienced a powerful homesickness to be with those two again, instead of here, back in the hotel.

None the less, Hannelore had looked a little less than straightforward as she pressed her clothes upon me. Sweet and kind as she was she had too much sense to lend one of her better things, and that endeared me to her still more, as if we were both sensible young *Mevrouen* who met most days in a house in the little street, and drank coffee, and gossiped with calm affection. My life was going to be far away from such a place, and already going who knows where; and it saddened me, and made me feel more than ever homesick: also more hostile than ever to Cloe and Charles.

Incidentally Hannelore and I had had a good laugh over the jeans she originally brought out to loan me. They were very much intended for her own ample form, and would have fallen straight off me. Even the waistband of the cotton skirt needed tucking up round me with safety pins.

I rambled on about my couple, hating to hear myself

doing so; and still Cloe said nothing. Nor did Charles. Did he know what she had been up to? He must do, surely. And yet how could one know? Had they determined to keep me out of something? In his own way Charles was so much under her thumb that if she had told him what she had got up to – something thoroughly discreditable perhaps – and told him to keep it dark from me, he would be as absurdly gratified as if she had promised to keep herself pure for him forever. On my reading of Charles, he would be like that. Tell him you had been unfaithful to him: but that you and he and nobody else would share the secret together, and he would be as pleased as a dog with two tails.

I hated showing my curiosity, but there seemed no other way to go about it. 'So what happened to you last night?' I demanded.

Cloe raised her eyebrows, as if in protest against the crudity of this direct approach. But she looked pleased with herself too: she had forced me to ask the question, and show openly that I was longing to hear what had happened to her.

She was still in no hurry to tell me. But then quite effortlessly she was telling me, between negligent sips at her coffee cup. And as she spoke I unexpectedly found myself becoming filled with a most murderous jealousy.

She was telling me that this very tall dark man – hadn't she seen me talking to him for a moment, at the edge of the dance floor? – had followed her after she found herself outside the town hall among the crowd of revellers, all more or less cheerfully drunk. It was clear that a good many of them had tried to get hold of her; but probably in so confused a fashion that she'd had little bother fending them off. They had been a happy bleary goodnatured crowd; and it seemed obvious that she had played the nymph among satyrs quite effectively by grabbing them all and kissing them back when they laid hold on her: in that way she had easily evaded any single one's pursuit.

But with the tall man it was different. Part of the trouble

had apparently been, to begin with anyway, that the crowd she was with had the idea that he was the one she fancied, and would be going off with in the end. And in fact, as they had all romped and halloed together along the streets, the tall man had managed eventually to isolate her. The others seemed to make off in different directions, and although she tried to run after a group of them the big man blocked her off. Then he'd suddenly seized hold of her and forced her into the mouth of a dark passageway. There was so much happy screaming and shouting going on that her own screams, however much more urgent they should have sounded to anyone still capable of telling the difference, could well have gone unremarked.

She'd tried to hit him and go for his privates, as Cloe rather quaintly put it, but he got hold of her wrists, and squeezing them tightly backed her into the darkest place by the inner wall.

Even Charles, who had presumably heard the story before, began to look rather uneasily spellbound at this point.

As for me, I found my fingers clenching and unclenching. My sore stomach felt empty, and full of hatred and nausea as well.

So my policeman had tried to rape Cloe. No doubt he had succeeded. No doubt, rather, that by a timely compliance she would have turned an attempted rape into a mutually satisfactory little grapple. If that were so, and I felt no doubt but that it was, Cloe showed not the least sign of haste or evasion as she approached with relish what must be the climax of her little drama.

I knew already how she was going to end it. But she took her time. She was enjoying describing her prolonged speechless determined struggle, culminating in the way she had eventually managed to scrape her high heel down his shin and instep, which must have really hurt him. With a curse he'd suddenly let go of her.

I liked the curse. A highly artistic touch. And then? Oh

well then of course she'd torn off as hard as she could go, pelting along the canal street; and her hat – my hat – came off as she ran and went into the canal. She was far too concerned with getting away to bother about that. Then she'd overtaken a young couple, by now fairly sober, who were on their way home. Overwrought as she was – Cloe spread her arms about in mock agitation to convey without shame or reserve the state she'd undoubtedly been in – she begged them to help her, indicating the presence of a per-haps still pursuing rapist somewhere behind, although in fact by that time no other person was visible in the street.

She was quite breathless of course, and when she man-aged to get out what had happened, and they had taken in her English, incoherent as it was as well as unfamiliar to them, they both became extremely indignant on her behalf. The honour of the streets of the Hague, of Holland itself, was at stake. They urged her to come with them to the police station, to describe her assailant and see whether he figured in the rogue's gallery of persons known to the police as robbers or molesters of young ladies. Cloe pronounced 'young ladies' in what she intended as the Dutch manner, assuming a droll expression to indicate the young persons' archaic vocabulary, no doubt imbibed from textbooks learnt at school.

At any rate she'd rejected out of hand the idea of going to the police station. 'Oh, then you missed an interesting expe-rience,' I interrupted at this point, with malice aforethought. 'Charles and I were there this morning enquiring after you; and the young officer was so helpful, and so handsome, wasn't he, Charles?'

Cloe ignored me. She'd felt quite knocked out, and the young couple had pressed her to come him with them – it was quite close. They had given her hot milk and brandy, and she had spent the rest of the night on their sofa very comfortable, covered in duvets. It had been nearly dawn by then, and she'd slept right through to one o'clock. They hadn't disturbed her.

Sweet resourceful indomitable little Cloe. Adventurous yes, but always prudent.

I knew she was lying. I knew what she had told me wasn't true. How did I know? I knew it as certainly as I could see my red hat floating in the canal.

Cloe had got off with my policeman; they'd spent the night together somewhere. And next day he'd come to me, and made love to me, and told me the story about the Israeli restaurant.

I hated her. But I didn't hate my policeman for what he had done. I loved him too much.

I realised just how much I loved him at that very moment.

'Well, isn't that funny,' I told her. 'I met this young couple too. The ones who leant me those clothes. They're coming tomorrow to collect them and bring back mine.' I paused, and then added deliberately: 'Wouldn't it be funny if they turned out to be the same young couple as the ones you spent the night with?'

'It would be a hoot,' said Charles gravely.

I gave him a sharp look. But his comment seemed quite harmless. Like so many experts (and I suppose one has to admit that he *does* know about painting) Charles, I decided, was at bottom a rather innocent sort of man.

Perhaps it's that which had made me fall a bit in love with him. Before I met my policeman.

There were no looks between Charles and Cloe. I think Charles believed her completely. Why should he not do so? It was because I knew my policeman that I didn't believe her. Charles was just grateful that she was back. He wasn't even too worried about the attempted rape. If no harm had been done, and Cloe shrugged the incident off as she seemed to have done, what was there for him to worry about? Cloe is not the sort of girl to bother with counselling and all that, although no doubt there is plenty of it in Holland.

He was just glad she was back; and I could see by the way he glanced at me occasionally that he hoped and expected I wasn't going to say anything indiscreet about what he had got up to with me when she was away. Attempted to get up to, that is.

Poor Charles. Why should I bother? He had enough on his hands now with Cloe herself; for I could see that her absence, and the story she had told to him – and now to me – had in some indefinable way greatly strengthened her hold over him.

I contemplated her with a hatred in my smile which she had, I hope, no means of detecting. What should I do? What could I do? My heart, or perhaps it was just my sore stomach, felt like lead.

For a moment I contemplated going and getting drunk on my own in the bar. On old Geneva. Or young Geneva – who cared which? But I knew it would only make me feel yet more miserable, and even more murderous. Muttering instead something about feeling tired and being off to bed, I left the pair of them. As I did so – it must have been caused by the interval of sitting down – I became painfully aware that the Dutch girl, however improbably, had much smaller feet than mine. The green suede shoes she'd lent me, no doubt an old pair she never wore now, had started to pinch like the devil, and I was conscious of shuffling most inelegantly across the carpet towards the lift.

Reaching it I looked back towards Charles and Cloe. Their heads were close together and they were deep in talk. Maybe about Vermeer; maybe about the shortcomings of the Dutch apple pie, and whether they should have gone out to find another restaurant, instead of sitting and waiting for me to show up: a girl who was, after all, perfectly capable of looking after herself.

I felt excluded and forlorn. For a moment I even found myself wondering if Cloe perhaps was telling the truth about what had happened to her last night. But I put that possibility resolutely away. In relation to my policeman, and in the way she must have made up to him after the dance, she bore all the signs of guilt. That was undeniable, at least for me.

And so a girl who was perfectly capable of looking after herself bent her steps towards that funny old Dutch lift.

I entered the little room it presented, and since no one else was around or appeared to want to use it as a lift, I sat down on the comfortable chair in the corner on which my policeman had originally been sitting. I felt slightly faint, and I wanted to get my bearings a bit. Where was my dear policeman now? If he had indeed gone off with Cloe, and I still felt pretty sure of that, what had happened to him since? He had betrayed me to the people in the restaurant, perhaps offering me up to the bronzed young man as some kind of reward for services rendered. I had evaded that at least. Perhaps, if he knew, my policeman would be annoyed with me for having put out his arrangements? The thought of his possible displeasure made me feel even more depressed.

And Cloe was the source of all the trouble. How, for a start, had she come to lose my hat, my red hat? It had fallen off, no doubt, when she was kissing him beside the canal. And where had my Lady Greensleeves tripped off to with him then? Not much grass around in the Hague, and somebody once told me that Greensleeves is really a bawdy song. Some young fellow who'd enjoyed the lady's favours hit on the nickname for her and it stuck – like the grassmarks on her elbows.

If I'm bitchy it must be the shock. I felt murderous and yet yearning at the same time. Yearning for my policeman, who had handed me over to his friends at the Israeli restaurant. Murderous at the thought of his walk-out with Cloe.

What did he think had happened to me? And where was he now?

I would find out. Somehow I would find him again, and

have it all out with him. And maybe fall into his arms. Would he reject me, now that he'd had Cloe?

Quite suddenly I had an idea. I would go down instead of up. It seemed appropriate somehow. And if my policeman was anywhere he might be lurking in the basement. True, I had been down there once before with him, sitting on his knee; and then there had seemed to be nothing but a blank wall; but why shouldn't I try again?

I pressed the brass button.

I was down there in no time; only it looked different. The open side of the lift now seemed to face a service door. Through it came muffled but emphatic noises: a banging of saucepans and plates, raucous cries and whistlings; a burst of uncouth laughter.

There was a metal bar running the width of the battered white door. I gave it a tentative push. It opened inwards at once, and so readily that I found myself halfway through it, and off balance. The light was brilliant and a great explosion of steam and clamour seemed to hit me in the face. There were figures in the misty confusion: huge old women in white, with mob caps on their heads and red arms like boiled lobsters. Nobody paid me any attention.

And then I saw him. He was standing in the background, by a door with a red light on outside it. His white overalls were dirty and dark red in places. He was leaning on a small two-wheeled barrow, the kind porters at the station used to have. Balanced on it was a sack of greens, and on top of that a great joint of raw meat. He had on a shapeless white cap, the same as those worn by the women.

At the moment I spotted him the red light went out; a door slid back and he lumbered inside with his barrow. The heavy-looking door slid shut. So concerned was I at his disappearance that I found myself taking several steps forward, almost into the middle of the kitchen. Still no one paid me any attention.

Then the door opened again and he came out, pushing his

now empty barrow. He skirted the kitchen area, coming in my direction, as if on his way to pick up another load. No doubt I was the last person he expected to see down there.

'Hallo, policeman,' I said.

He didn't look a bit surprised; I will say that. I never really felt prouder of him than I did at that moment. He stopped and smiled at me, leaning on the handles of his barrow.

'Remember me?' I went on. 'Your junior colleague, sort of. Reporting for duty.'

He still said nothing. By now I was back in the lift, hardly conscious of how I'd got there. He'd followed me in, still smiling at me, and now he pressed one of the buttons. As the lift began to rise, in its slow majestic fashion, he peeled off his bloodstained overalls and stuffed then through the opening just as the lift, in rising, closed it off.

He still said nothing, and I felt I had no more to say, but our silence seemed peaceful. The lift stopped at my floor, the top one, and I walked out without looking at him. I could feel him following behind me.

Reaching my door I automatically felt for my bag to get out the card to open the door. No bag of course: therefore no card. My bag must be still somewhere upstairs, at the Israeli restaurant.

I felt weightless for a moment, and quite lost. I found myself leaning helplessly against the door.

Then a big dark hand reached out from behind me. A card went into the slot, and the door opened.

Some time later, when we were in bed, I found myself wondering how I was going to get my passport back, and the air ticket home. As it was a quiet moment I mentioned this to him. He told me not to worry. He would arrange it all.

'Your work was good,' he said into my ear as I settled against him. 'Better than you know'.

I know I blushed with pleasure, probably all over. What reply could I make to such praise?

Having received it I snuggled into him and dozed off at

once. I had not demanded an explanation of why he had sent me to the Israeli restaurant, let alone reproached him about it. Nor, needless to say, had I said a word about Cloe, and my suspicions about the previous night. I had taken him back and asked no questions. As soon as he had come up to my room with me everything was as it should be again.

Except for one thing. When I woke up again – it must have been only a few minutes after I had drifted off to sleep, I found him starting to strangle me.

Sounds dramatic, doesn't it? Well, it wasn't, actually. When I say that he was starting to strangle me I don't mean that I knew at the time that this was what he was doing. One hardly expects such a thing, does one, even from a tall dark kitchen porter who says he is an Israeli policeman, with whom one has fallen in love?

In fact I had been having vivid dreams, which now seemed to mingle rather pleasantly, in the way dreams do, with the sensations I was experiencing. They had not been so much dreams as vivid recollections, which may show that I had barely been asleep at all, but in a pre-sleep drowse. The first was of the picture by Vermeer I had seen the day before yesterday (how long ago it seemed): the one of the female saint who is wringing out the martyr's blood into a basin. How absorbed in it she had seemed, like that later study of the sturdy woman pouring her thin stream of milk. My little Dutch girl, the half of the young couple who had brought me home, would look very like that in a year or two's time – like the milk-pouring woman I mean. The female saint, in her mystic absorption, was quite different; but something in the nature of her task made me now wonder whether her colleague with the milk-jug might not be engaged in an activity more complex than just pouring milk: could she be trying to separate it in some way from some other substance lurking in the jug? We shall never know.

These dreamy speculations seemed to go with a more positive and recent event: what would happen to the bloodstained overall my porter had so deftly cast from the side of the lift, as we ascended: and what would his colleagues in that steamy underworld feel about his sudden and unexplained departure from duty? All these thoughts, or pictures, seemed to mingle in my mind as if in a dance with the comfort of the warm massive creature I was cuddled against, and with the way that his hands were holding and caressing my throat.

I found out all about strangulation later on – post-operatively, one might say. The word suggests something disagreeable; far from painless, possibly even agonising. But don't you believe it. I should like to put my findings at the service of the League for Capital Punishment, if there is such a thing. The only really good argument against hanging is the way it is done. The 'humane' way, so called, with a long drop and a broken neck. It was much kinder when they just left you to dangle. How so? I can safely aver from my own experience that the victim would have known absolutely nothing about it. He would have been happily unconscious within seconds, though maybe not absolutely dead for some time after that.

I don't know just how long after; because of course I wasn't absolutely dead myself, although I must have been pretty near it. I was certainly becoming unconscious. The first I knew was this banging on the door; and that must have been when my policeman or porter removed his hand, and the blood started to flow again to my head along the carotid artery (I got all these technical terms later on).

That's all he'd really been doing, caressing my throat, and giving it a little love squeeze just in the right place. It was heaven as I drifted off, and he must have known that. Plenty of experience probably. It was just like going to sleep, breathing quite naturally, and feeling his big chest against me as I breathed. Quite a *Liebestod*, really.

But then there had come this most unwelcome knocking

at the door, and in a second he was gone from me. I was conscious of that, just as I was of the insistent knocking.

What happened then? Oh, such an anticlimax. It was Cloe at the door. She told me all about it as we sat together on my bed, later on. Or rather she told me her own version of the story, and why she'd come upstairs and started banging on my door.

She was anxious about me – that's why. Or that was what she said. Cloe – anxious about me! If you believe that, you'd believe anything.

And why should she have been anxious about me? Because of my adventure of the evening, and falling into the canal, and all that? Well, that was what she said.

And, of course, it could just have been true. At this distance in time I'm prepared to admit that.

But if it were true, by any chance, why does Cloe say nothing now about how she found me in bed with my porter, and what happened to him?

Me? Well, I'm a casualty, though neither of us was prepared to recognise that. 'You were so fast asleep,' she said. 'It was really difficult to wake you up.'

Nothing about why she had needed to wake me up. Instead of leaving a poor girl to have her beauty sleep undisturbed. She had been worried because she found the outer door not quite shut properly. She knocked a few times, and then came in to make sure I hadn't caught a sudden chill from my immersion, or was suffering from secondary shock, and lying insensible. Anxious, careful, compassionate Cloe.

So what did happen? That's pretty clear – wouldn't you say? At least to me. The night before my porter had asked her about me; had even hinted, or boasted, of the time he'd already had with me. Cloe was jealous. She had been in his arms somewhere. Perhaps in some secret unknown room in the hotel itself, to which our porter, in his usual way, had acquired access? When I came in, as she and Charles were having dinner, she was convinced I'd been with her burly boyfriend. Perhaps I was going to see him again in my room that night?

Consumed with jealousy Cloe waits awhile, perhaps till after Charles has gone to sleep. Then she comes up to me to make sure nothing's going on. And there's plenty going on.

Her story about the door being slightly open. Rubbish. Of course our porter shut it most effectively. Everything like that he does so well.

Cloe knocked so long and so persistently on the door because she was more and more determined to discover if he was in there. All the same it must have been a shock for her to find that he was.

Did he just brush past her, in his shirt and trousers, as he swiftly and suddenly opened the door? Or did he pause for a moment, kiss her, even instruct her, in the way he does so well, about another meeting, in another place, later on?

No way of knowing. I was dead to the world for all practical purposes. So I shall never know. And, naturally enough, Cloe has no intention of ever telling me, any more than I will ever tell her how I came to be in bed with a man – her man, our man – when she had run up the stairs to knock with determination on my door.

Cloe was truthful about one thing. I must have been in a state of shock, even though I had no awareness of the fact. And I suppose I continued to be so for some time. After all one can hardly be half strangled, misleading as I have shown that term to be, without feeling some after-effects. Of course I began to wonder, some time later on, if he had already tried it out on Cloe; but at that time I was coming back to myself I have to admit that I was just glad of her company, and her ministrations.

In fact she insisted on spending the night – the rest of the night – in my room. I had no objections. I was too dazed to care, one way or another; but I wonder now whether she was not taking her own precautions against our porter coming back. Out of jealousy? Well, perhaps; but Cloe is a human

96

being, when all's said and done, and she knew – must have known – what had happened. Perhaps the same thing had happened, or nearly happened, to her the night before? Looking back it seems quite possible. Her own passion might well have been tempered by some degree of apprehension; and she felt we had better stay together for mutual support. Just in case anything further did happen.

So she rang down to Charles and told him I wasn't very well, and she felt she ought to stay with me. Most hotel singles, even on the top floor, have a second bed in case they need to become doubles. The other bed wasn't made up, but Cloe found enough blankets and things in the cupboard. She made herself a nest quite rapidly and dexterously while I sat in a stupor, feeling occasionally impelled to shake my head gently from side to side.

She glanced at me once or twice while I was doing this, and asked if I was sure I felt all right. I said I did. Did Cloe know already what it was like to be amorously strangled by our policeman porter? Had she stopped him somehow, whereas I had happily sailed off into that unconsciousness which, if it hadn't been for her knocking on the door, could well have been permanent? Except that I'm sure he'd have revived me just in time.

I was certainly glad to have Cloe there, really glad; and all the more because after I had at last got to sleep I woke with a nightmare at what must have been two or three o'clock. As I woke it was, or became, a waking nightmare. I was sure he was still in the room, or had got back into the room. I was convinced of it.

I lay tense, listening. Which of us would he go for first, since he must be in a state of frustration about being interrupted when – as it were – nearly there with me? How near had he come, the previous night, to throttling Cloe? Or hadn't he even tried? I couldn't help hoping, even at that moment, that I had been the one he wanted to do it to.

Of course sensible little Cloe had checked the outer door

with care. But she didn't know about the card trick our policeman porter was able to play on the door. It was I who knew that he could come in, to do what he wanted, at any hour of the night. Or the day for that matter.

And here we were in such a nice quiet cosy and comfortable old-fashioned Dutch hotel. The very last place you would expect to get into trouble of this sort. I started to wonder, at about four o'clock, if it had ever happened there before – or nearly happened. It would be case of heart failure I suppose; or I believe young people can be found dead in the morning from a sort of grown-up equivalent of cot death. They might have been single women, of various ages, who had come to see the Vermeers?

A displeasing thought: highly displeasing. If anyone is going to be murdered in our hotel, and by the policeman porter, it ought to be me, and me only. He belonged to me. He was my policeman. Had he really intended to strangle me? Quite likely not; and it had certainly felt so soothing, even delicious, like some new way of making love. (It was only when I read up about it afterwards that I saw how close to death I must have been.) But of course I was frightened, because he really *might* have been trying to kill me. How should I know?

These were the thoughts that went round and round in my head. Did I find myself wondering also if the Dutch used the same sort of expressions which our caring professions go in for? No doubt our friend was traumatised, or pathologically challenged in some way. Had he at some point been 'released into the community', and a job found for him at the hotel?

The morning came at last, and Cloe and I were still unmolested. Was I the tiniest bit sorry that our man had not returned? Certainly I had spent the last hour before the dawn wondering how I should, as it were, receive him if he did. I knew what I felt about him. And that helped to keep me awake too, I suppose.

When the light came in I got up, had a shower and put on my spare pair of trousers. I found a laundry bag and parcelled up the Dutch girl's belongings as best I could. Cloe remained, or pretended to remain, resolutely asleep. I sat on my bed, determined to say nothing to her about what had happened in the night; and I think she must have come to the same decision, for when she suddenly sat up, swung her short legs out of bed – she was wearing her slip and blouse – and scuttled into the bathroom, she did so in a sort of forgiving silence. Was she in two minds as well as me about the fact that our policeman porter had not returned? But then I reflected that she had made quite sure the door of our room was locked; and she must have been confident that even if he prowled about in the passage he couldn't get in.

Whatever their last night's relationship had been, she may well have taken fright when she saw what had happened to me. It may have taken me a minute or so to return to consciousness, and a lesser girl would have panicked. No doubt she didn't want the hotel people, and possibly an ambulance, and even the police, any more that I did. She had seen her man at the door, after all, as he fled from the room. And after reviving me she may well have realised that she might herself have been lucky to survive the previous night.

So in sober silence we went down to breakfast together. Cloe had rung Charles, and he joined us eventually, after we had already consumed a good deal of cheese, smoked salmon and cold roast beef. I was extremely hungry, which was natural enough as I'd had no supper; but Cloe for some reason seemed equally voracious. Disappointed love perhaps?

I'd left the package of clothes at reception, asking them to direct the girl to the dining room if she arrived; but when I went back after breakfast it was to find that the girl had indeed called in, no doubt on her way to work, and had left my clothes, which turned out to have been beautifully ironed and pressed when I opened the parcel upstairs.

I had been told by the man at reception that the girl had apologised for not coming in, but had said she was already late for work. No doubt the invitation into the dining-room had made her feel timid. I was really sorry not to see her, though I did at least have her name and address. I should have liked to confront her with Cloe, just on the off-chance that they might have met after the dance: even the off-chance that Hannelore and her boyfriend had been the very pair on whose sofa Cloe had – allegedly – spent the night, or rather the morning after. If that had turned out to be the case I'm fair-minded enough, I hope, to admit that I should have had to change my ideas about Cloe and her recent conduct.

But in another way I was glad to have kept my little Dutch couple to myself. I wouldn't like Cloe to have known them, still less Charles. They belonged to me, and to what had happened to me. They were a little place of peace and affection; even though I was still very sure I'd had to share my *real* experiences here at the Hague with bloody Cloe. A thoroughly humiliating thought.

No matter. It was over now. Over for her at least, if not for me. We packed up, paid the bill – I promising Charles my share in the form of a cheque when we got home, since I had lost my handbag in the canal. The friendly hotel people had already told me there would be no immediate worry about the loss of my passport. They had informed the police, and I had been issued through the hotel with a certificate of my residence there which would satisfy the authorities at Schipol and Heathrow.

It was a nuisance to end on, but also a fitting distraction. Charles and Cloe were arguing about taking a taxi all the way to Amsterdam, or merely using one to catch the train that goes there. Which would be the quicker, to get them to the Rijksmuseum? Charles maintained the saving of time in going by taxi would more than compensate for the increase in cost. Cloe vigorously demurred. They already sounded like a married couple.

It was a foggy morning, and the crocuses looked damp and sleek in the grass in front of the hotel. Taxis were there; and Charles went forward through the murk to make arrangements with one that might be amenable to either of their plans. Cloe and I waited with the suitcases. There seemed nothing to say. Normally, I suppose, we should have chattered away as friends do at the end of an excursion, recalling the big moments, minor disappointments, things that had made us laugh. So we stood there in a polite silence; each wondering, I suppose, what the other was thinking about the events that had taken place.

A big man loomed suddenly up beside us, a big dark man. He stood in front of me, bowing. Then he took my hand, raised it to his lips and kissed it. Continuing to hold it he gave me my handbag, and with it a parcel, neatly done up. Releasing my hand he produced a red rose and fastened it with a safety pin to the front of my coat. I tucked my handbag and the parcel under my arm as he did so. Then he took both my hands, leant down, and kissed me on the mouth. He straightened up to attention, gave what I suppose was a click of the heels, though quite noiselessly, and went off into the fog.

It had taken less than a minute. I turned to look at Cloe, whom the man had ignored as if she wasn't there. Cloe's face had gone red, as red as the rose. We still said nothing, and it was only a few seconds before Charles arrived with the taxi.

All the discussion made no difference in the end, because before we reached the Rijksmuseum Cloe was ill. No question about putting it on either: she was really ill. Perhaps food poisoning, perhaps a sudden kind of 'flu, or something more personal than that. She suffered mutely. Charles was worried and solicitous and ineffectual; I was just ineffectual. The question was would she be able to fly that evening. In the end she was. So we all got back to London.

I rang Cloe up next day of course. She was much better. We agreed to meet. We haven't met. I don't suppose we shall meet now, but I shall send her these pages I am writing before I go back. That way she will know that I think about it all, and what my suspicions are. She may find the whole thing double-Dutch, but I don't think so.

Where am I going back to? To the hotel of course, and to my man, my policeman porter. What will happen there? I've no idea. For all I know he may really work for the Israelis, or the Palestinians, or both. The porter job would be good cover I suppose. And funny things may really go on at the restaurant. By coincidence I read this morning in the paper that the Dutch authorities had expelled as suspected terrorists some Palestinians living in the Hague.

Alternatively, of course, the whole thing is nonsense, my man a mere maniac, with a mind full of fantasy, and a lethal obsession. Well, whichever it is, I'm going to find out.

Oh, incidentally, the parcel he handed me right at the end – guess what was in it? Yes, you're right, Cloe, it was a red hat. A much more beautiful hat than the one you did for me. Goodness knows where he bought it, or got hold of it. It's black velvet lined with white silk, under the red plumes. I put it on every evening in the flat and look at myself in the mirror. I'd thought of sending it to you, Cloe, before I go, as a sort of consolation prize. But now I think not. No, I shall take it with me on my journey back to him.

II

People like pictures, if they do, for all sorts of different reasons. I personally find something rather sympathetic in Nancy Deverell's attitude to them, as revealed in the account of her adventures despatched, no doubt with some malice aforethought, to Cloe Winterbotham. Cloe is quite a good friend of mine, as well as a very old friend, having regard to our respective ages; and it appears she is in the same sense an old friend of Nancy Deverell, or at least the latter appears to have thought of her as such. I wouldn't know, never having met this Nancy, but I am beginning to hope that I may presently do so.

Cloe is eight or nine years younger than me: a different generation in a sense, although women marry men ten years older than themselves all the time, even in this day and age. I don't exactly think I ever wanted to marry Cloe; I would, all the same, dearly have loved to have an affair with her. That, alas, did not happen, despite my best efforts. 'You're so oldfashioned, Roland,' she used to say. 'Even your name is oldfashioned, though that's one of the things I like about it, and about you.' But she didn't like it, or me presumably, enough to respond in the way I was hoping. I sometimes wonder who she does like to go to bed with.

Perhaps she's too fond of herself to fancy either men or women? But it looks as if she may favour gay men who have decided by an exercise of the will to go straight for a while, or even to settle down in a nice comfortable double life. Charles Martin for example. Even as I write she is on the verge of marriage with Charles, and I have been asked to the wedding. I trust my old friend status will remain unimpaired. I rather fancy it will be. Cloe is very dependent on her friends, because she knows how to make use of them.

She is certainly making use of me, and I love it. It would be hard to say just why – just why she is making use of me I mean. I love it for my own reasons.

Charles? Well I have mixed feelings about him. Perhaps that's only to be expected. Undoubtedly he is a very able fellow, although he is the opposite of the sort of clean-cut image that phrase suggests. As Nancy Deverell accepts, or at least seems to take for granted, he really is good on pictures, although Vermeer is not his special study: I rather fancy it may be Tiepolo. He is Professor of Fine Art at London; an OK job I should imagine as regards the money, and I believe he has plenty of his own. That may be one of the reasons Cloe is marrying him. She never has much; and, oddly enough for such an attractive and apparently competent girl, she never seems to hold down a decent job. She's always on the move, usually doing something secretarial at an art gallery, which must be how she first met Charles.

I'd assumed that Cloe's comparative penury would be a help to me in my seducing project? I took her out to good restaurants and always paid. I enjoyed doing it too, because spending a certain amount of money is fun when you have come into it unexpectedly, as I did. I used to be a sort of poor man's academic, teaching English at one of the small London colleges, near Ealing. After the windfall from an aunt I'd barely met since I was a little boy, I had no hesitation in giving it up. Aunt Joan must have liked me once, or at least could think of no one else to leave her money to: fortunately she'd always had a strong aversion to domestic pets. Lived very quietly, and had a really surprising amount invested.

Unquestionably Cloe liked me and made use of me because I was well off; and I revelled in that. There was not much else to revel in, but never mind. I like leisure, especially after ten years or so of hard teaching; but, as somebody says in Oscar Wilde, a young man – a comparatively young man in my case – must have something to do, even if it's only smoking cigarettes, which of course has to be done out in the street these days. Knowing Cloe gave me something to do: a good deal to do in fact. Cloe made good use of her *Cavaliere servente* – getting the smoked salmon from Sainsbury's and supplying the wine if she had friends to dinner – and her patronage gave me the reputation of being a 'kind' man.

Perhaps I really am a kind man? I wouldn't know. I like being kind to Cloe anyway: it's the next best thing to being able to go to bed with her. But I really think, having read her story, that I may soon be transferring my kindness fund to Nancy Deverell. I was struck by her tale of events – it turned out to be a long letter to Cloe really – to the point of wishing with what for me is quite remarkable intensity to get to know this peculiar girl.

A Red Hat girl, as she constantly calls herself. I wouldn't know about that: I've never even seen the picture. She makes it sound quite striking, I'll say that. And Cloe tells me Nancy Deverell, whom she has known in a vague way for a longish time, is indeed rather a peculiar girl – 'if you can call Nance a girl at all', said Cloe with a laugh. She refused to be more specific than that, and soon I discovered why. Cloe wanted to make use of me, as has done so many times, but in a distinctly unusual context.

'Roland?' she asked. 'Could you find Nancy, do you think? Would you mind having a try?'

She had paved the way, as it were, for this request by giving me 'this dotty document' to read. 'It certainly is dotty, but it's also rather fascinating,' she said to tempt me; and when I'd read it I saw all too clearly what she meant, and I had to agree with her.

I could also see, or thought I could see, why she wanted me to find Nancy. It was not just out of pique, or curiosity. Cloe herself gets a fairly tough going-over in Nancy's account of their stay at the Hague; and I was deeply gratified, indeed touched, by the fact that she didn't mind me seeing what Nancy had written about her. In some ways, of course, her attitude is a kind of insult, as if she were saying: 'Roland means so little to me that I don't care what he thinks.' A lot of men would object to that. But it doesn't worry me a bit. On the contrary.

Much more important is the fact that Cloe is genuinely worried about Nancy Deverell. I'm sure of that. The most unlikely people have a streak of caringness, as I suppose it has to be called today, and I have formed the impression that without wanting to say so, or in any way to go on about it, Cloe feels protective about Nancy Deverell. She may have saved her life after all, or at least Nancy seems to have thought said so – I'll return to that in a minute – and Somerset Maugham says somewhere that it's easy to get away from friends who've done you a good turn, but surprisingly difficult to drop people whom you've been kind to yourself. The old cynic ought to have known I suppose.

Anyway, when I asked Cloe, as delicately as I could, if there was any truth at all in Nancy's highly-coloured account of the things that had happened to the three of them at the Hague, I was surprised by the manner in which she received my query. Of course I had put my own question the other way round, pretending to take it for granted that this Nancy must be a fantasist of the most comprehensive kind, working off some sort of spite against Cloe by sending her this admittedly rather fascinating piece of invention. I went on to pooh-pooh the notion that there could be anything in it that was even remotely true, except no doubt the time spent at the exhibition, and perhaps the fancy-dress dance at the Town Hall.

Cloe tapped her teeth thoughtfully against the glass of pink gin she was holding. She only likes one drink in the evening but she likes a strong one: Bombay gin, the smoothest and most expensive kind, with which I supply her. She was condescending to give me a supper of some sort that evening, because she wanted to talk about Nancy's manuscript 'letter'. Now she had an unusually responsible air.

'Is that what you really think?' she said, when I had

finished dismissing Nancy's ramblings as the day-dreams of an odd and no doubt unsatisfied young woman.

'Well, don't you?'

'Not really, no.'

It suits Cloe's femaleness to appear enigmatic, which she now did to some effect.

I was surprised none the less that she was prepared to concede the idea, having regard to what Nancy Deverell had written about her presumed relations with the mystery man referred to by Nancy as 'my policeman' or 'my policeman porter'. Although my own attitude of total scepticism was in a sense put on to be tactful, it really did seem to me wildly unlikely that there could be any truth in the story. Episodes like that in the lift or in the bedroom just don't happen; and particularly not, I should have thought, in a respectable Dutch hotel. Real life surely doesn't oblige in such a way?

It's true that Nancy's sprightly account did give these events a certain plausibility. I had been particularly struck by the meeting in the lift, and what had taken place there. And yet if there was this strange oldfashioned lift at the hotel, and a man once happened to have been sitting in a corner of it, what more likely than that Nancy's obviously lively imagination should have done the rest? There was a waif-like and rather desperate charm about the way she wrote which suggested an inner loneliness, a longing to find something or someone to love: a loneliness no doubt exacerbated by the company of Cloe and Charles. Perhaps she had found that something by making up the very story she had written? It was a fantasy that could include her grudge against Cloe: her resentment against her friend Cloe's possession of Charles, and Cloe's so effortlessly being what she is.

But I was on tricky ground here. Supposing Cloe really had gone absent, and Nancy and Charles really had gone to the police station, what followed from that? Was Cloe's account in the story of what had happened – the man pursuing her after the dance, and her escape from him with the young Dutch couple – could that be true? What about Charles' attempt to make love to Nancy in Cloe's absence? In the circumstances there seemed nothing inherently improbable about that either.

For if any one part of the story was true, might there not be some truth in the rest of it too? Or was the whole plausibility of such a narrative founded on the fairly obvious principle that a little bit of circumstantial truth will cover up for a lot of lies? After all, I had been adding my own sort of 'truth', in a rather pompous way, by surmising that the real fact of the matter was Nancy's own needs and personality. If one understands Nancy, then her story makes its own kind of sense.

Cloe was eyeing me quizzically over her drink. I could see that she was wondering about what I thought of her role in Nancy's tale. Was she now going to tell me what had really happened, at least to her? But she didn't do that.

Nor did I feel disposed to ask. Partly out of natural diffidence; but more, I think, because the idea of Nancy Deverell had really taken possession of me. I wanted very much to meet her, to find things out from her. The true facts. No doubt it was naive to suppose she would tell me what had really taken place; and yet why not, if I could present myself as a well-intentioned stranger? I was already and instinctively making up a plan of campaign.

Cloe must have seen all this. She is no intellectual, but I have always admired her speed of intuition, which is far greater than my own. She can adapt in a flash, and present her chosen victims – Charles for instance – with what they are up to before they know it themselves. She has turned herself now, I notice, into what is virtually a super-Charles, behind whom the real Charles has to run to keep up. She's displaced him with what she's decided he shall be, and he is grateful for it: he admires the idea of himself that she holds up to him.

But what about Nancy? I think from her account that Nancy had sized up Cloe pretty well, and it had given my friend a bit of a jolt to find that out. As long as she'd known Nancy she must have patronised her, in the almost but not quite invisible ways that come naturally to Cloe; and now she wanted me to help her restore Nancy to that patronage. But I concede that there is more to it than that. Cloe, as I have said, has kindly impulses, almost inseparable from her possessive ones; and I'm inclined to think these are what were really inducing her to seek out Nancy, and to succour her if need be.

Of course this in itself implied that Cloe believed at least some parts of Nancy's story. Why otherwise should Nancy be in need of help, even of rescue? I had started by assuming that Nancy, always it seemed a loner and a wanderer by temperament, had simply abandoned whatever contacts in London she had in common with Cloe, and gone off somewhere on her own. From wherever it was she had written her 'story', or fantasy, and fired it off at her friend. I had the feeling, after reading it, that this idea had only occurred to her some time after she had begun writing, perhaps as part of a deliberate sensation or climax. The earlier part, thumbing her nose at Vermeer and the picture gallery, enjoying feeling superior to her stuffy companions, imagining herself as the girl in the Red Hat, was, I thought, simply a way to amuse herself: perhaps a rather forlorn and lonely way.

'So did she look like the Girl in the Red Hat?' I found myself saying: and I'm sure that query, too, Cloe had anticipated.

'Not really, I think,' she replied as if judiciously. 'We said that to please her. The girl in the hat could be anyone really; and say what you like about Nancy, she's quite an individual.'

I saw her point. Nancy had not only exaggerated her own likeness to the Red Hat girl, but had emphasised that anyone familiar with the picture, particularly Charles and Cloe,

111

would be amazed at the resemblance. It was what had first caught the attention of the 'tall dark man' in the Gallery, the man whom she had presumably decided would be the one to play a part in her lift fantasy, and in the subsequent goings-on in bed.

About all that I was definitely disinclined to ask questions.

The fact is, I suppose, that I was already falling a little in love with Nancy. Or rather, it would be more accurate to say, with the image I had formed of her. But what's the difference? At any rate I was not only reluctant to question Cloe about the events in Nancy's story, the more peculiar events that is: I was just as reluctant to question myself too closely on what I felt about them. I think I must be one of those men – I've no idea how common or uncommon they are – who in spite of all the evidence cannot really bring themselves to believe in the unchastity of women; or perhaps I should rather say in their commonplace and, as it were, banally masculine sexual drives: what makes them from time to time desire a man as a man desires a woman. And although I didn't suppose there was any basic difference between Nancy Deverell and other women, I still preferred to believe that some things at least in her story could not possibly be true.

But I was not so much falling in love with Nancy, as I can now see, as with the story itself. It fascinated me to the point of wanting to continue it, to make up my own story about it, to muscle in on it in some way; though I have to admit that the idea of any activity requiring muscle power might seem a bit incongruous with my temperament and lifestyle.

The point is, however, that I was beginning to feel about Nancy in much the same way that Nancy felt about herself: that is to say, as a girl in a Red Hat. Or maybe as a boy. Any uncertainty on that point, whether in relation to her own feelings or to the portrait by Vermeer itself, seemed to give her pleasure.

What gave me pleasure was the idea of her story and mine getting together in some way. I was accustomed to oblige Cloe, and indeed enjoyed doing it, but I doubt if I should have taken on this assignment – I doubt it very much – if I hadn't been so intrigued by the figure of Nancy Deverell. So much so that when I got home that evening I at once began to make some notes on the story, of which I had made a copy, and even found myself beginning to write something of my own as if I was in touch with her. These attempts at a 'letter' to her were discarded later; and yet I did indeed begin to compose my reflections on the situation – some of which are present in revised form in this narrative – before I actually encountered Nancy.

But I anticipate. Cloe had something more to tell me, and to show me, that evening.

Over the prawn cocktail and the takeaway chicken – Cloe has strangely conventional ideas about what to give a guest for supper, or probably she just finds it easier to buy things from what must surely be a very oldfashioned delicatessen – she let me know everything that might be a help in my quest for Nancy, or at least everything that she was prepared to divulge. In a sense it wasn't a great deal, not really so very much more than what I had already picked up from Nancy's story. I commented on this, as tactfully as possible, and enquired how Cloe proposed that I should set about finding Nancy, when there was nothing more to go on than her own statement that she would soon be setting out on a 'journey back to him': that is to say to the fantasy figure whom she claimed to have met in the Hague. Was I to go to the Dutch capital and make enquiries at the hotel, or at the 'Israeli' restaurant? (This last clearly existed in some form, for Cloe had told me as much, and described the egregious meal she and Charles and Nancy had eaten there.)

'That won't be necessary,' said Cloe calmly.

'Why not?'

'I've had a letter from her.'

113

Cloe had kept this to the dessert, of chocolate eclairs with an obvious deli hallmark, and it aroused all my curiosity afresh.

'You mean a letter following up the long one she sent you?'

Cloe looked cross at that. She got her bag and took a postcard out of it, which she handed to me. Then she helped herself to another eclair.

I remembered Nancy Deverell's comment that Cloe would grow fat before she reached her middle years; and that, for some reason, made me feel all affectionate and loyal towards her. Amorous as well. I would have liked at least to have given her a kiss.

But this was obviously not the moment. I put the postcard down on the table without looking at it. That gave me a slight revenge for Cloe's look of crossness. But I had already seen it was a picture card covered with a few words in a sprawling handwriting. It was hardly a letter, although it must have been sent inside an envelope.

'So not from the Hague,' I stated. 'Where was it then?'

Cloe seemed to have decided to play this revelation in sibylline silence. Either that or she had already lost interest, and was contemplating seeing Charles next day, or perhaps some other admirer. She fished in her bag again and found a limp envelope, which she chucked across the table.

I picked it up, saw the French stamps, and looked at the smudgy postmark. The town or village was illegible, but below it I could just make out what seemed to be 'B du R.'

I know France reasonably well. The card had come from the Bouches du Rhône, the big district in the south above and to the west of Marseille.

'Don't worry,' said Cloe annoyingly, after I had worked this out. 'The name of the village, or whatever it is, is on the card.'

So it was – 'Mouriez'. And a date too, about three weeks before.

After that there was nothing for it but to read the card.

'Darling Cloe' it began, the two words taking up a lot of space, and contriving somehow to suggest a good deal of that mixture of malice, dependency and critical appraisal which animated the long fantasy from Nancy which had apparently turned into a letter. In the two words there even seemed to me to be something of the elfin self-indulgence on which Nancy evidently prided herself, almost as if she were mocking Cloe with a cliché that none the less still continued to hold out the promise of true affection and warmth.

Living in this charming spot at the moment. Country much more romantic than good old Holland. Would suit you and Charles for a holiday some time. Give him my love. And don't forget me. Nance.

'May I take this away?' I said at once. The richness of implication in that postcard, coming after my reading of Nancy's letter-fantasy, was indescribable.

'Do what you like,' said Cloe, as if wearying of the whole business, which she very likely had.

By 'richness' I mean the sheer variety of possibilities that seemed to lie in ambush in the card: for Cloe as its recipient, but now still more for me, as the agent hired to take over. (Yes: I decided as I pondered the matter later on that evening, after I had got home, that Cloe's chief purpose – I don't say her only one – had been to shift the burden of responsibility on to somebody else's shoulders.) The 'Darling Cloe' I continued to find touching. It was so much what every girl would write; and yet there seemed to be in it, at least for me, a wholly personal note of supplication; for a kind of comradeship, even for forgiveness. As if the fantasy letter itself had been no more, but no less either, than an appeal to an intimate to share one of their private jokes.

Had the joke misfired? I thought it more likely that Nancy, for all that she so obviously prided herself on her shrewd assessment of other people, had quite misjudged Cloe. Cloe didn't go in for jokes, private or otherwise. And wasn't there a hint in the last words of the card than Nancy herself recognised that? 'Don't forget me' – startling in its abrupt change of the holiday postcard tone, really meant 'it's no good my asking you not to ignore my existence, in spite of that long thing I sent you'.

Nancy may have thought she was in love with Charles. But I was beginning to wonder whether that she was not really a bit in love with Cloe.

Wouldn't that explain the creation of a fantasy figure, her tall policeman, when Cloe was doubly inaccessible through being absent? And mightn't it account for the fact, however much Nancy had played it down, that the real climax of her adventure had been the night with Cloe in her room? Although I had been discreet, or cowardly, in not asking her the more obvious questions, I'd had my query about that answered by Cloe. Yes, she had spent that night, the last of their stay, with Nancy. Nancy had been out wandering about somewhere, got wet, and seemed so down and depressed – frightened too – that when she'd burst into tears on Cloe's bosom and asked her to stay the night in the hotel room, Cloe of course had not had the heart to refuse.

That at least sounded true. Nancy's jealousy of her friend – 'murderous jealousy' she had written on one occasion – might well have been jealousy about Charles, as Cloe's more or less successful lover, soon perhaps to be husband. The passions can be transposed or transmogrified, as Nancy had apparently treated them in her 'story', but they always exist, and continue to exist: whereas politics and morality and that kind of thing are mainly a matter of passing fashion, the 'correctness' of the moment. True art, like passion, is equally permanent; and I suppose Vermeer's Red Hat picture, of which at the time I had not seen even a reproduction, existed for Nancy as it were alongside her passion, whoever that passion may have been for. She had evidently convinced

116

herself that a Red Hat girl must be worthy of the picture's own kind of promise.

Setting aside what still seemed to me the obvious if lively inventions of Nancy's tale, I remained curious about one specific thing, about which I felt none the less that I could hardly ask; notwithstanding the fact that it did not concern Cloe as directly as did most of what Nancy had made up about her. If Charles were gay, as I had always taken for granted, even though on the barest acquaintance, where did that put Cloe, and her plans for them both?

As it happened I needn't have been delicate about it, because it was Cloe herself who brought up the question.

'One of Nancy's wilder ideas seems to be that Charles is gay', she remarked. She probably thinks all arts people are. She's naive in many ways is our Nance.'

I decided that 'naive' was not exactly the word I would apply to the girl who had written that bizarre account of her time at the Hague; but I made no comment.

'She's a bit of a waif,' Cloe went on. 'Only child and never got on with either of her parents. Mother's dead. She married a Frenchman after divorcing Nancy's father. Father's now in California or somewhere. Odd man by all accounts, but quite rich. Nancy never seemed short of money.'

I wondered if her friend's comparative affluence had been one reason for Cloe's keeping up the relationship. But I was touched, too. What she told me seemed to indicate a greater degree of understanding of the other girl than Cloe had shown before, even a certain kind of protectiveness.

When I got home that evening I jotted some things down; and pondered the situation with, I must confess, a certain relish. Cloe had seemed to take it for granted that there could be no connection between Nancy's present location and the events she described as taking place in the Hague. I was not so sure. Given Cloe's more or less perfunctory account of what had really happened on their trip together, the implications of that postcard continued to intrigue me. The word

117

'living' somehow seemed unusual. Wouldn't the normal thing to write have been 'staying'? Why should Nancy have been 'living' in what must admittedly be, as I knew myself, an attractive area for visitors and tourists, if the word didn't suggest something more domestic than a mere visit, however protracted. Didn't it in fact suggest that she was living *with* somebody?

Her mother, who had divorced and married a Frenchman, was dead. So the commonplace explanation must be that she was living – but again, surely, 'staying' would have been the word? – with friends or relations by marriage. I continued to feel that she probably wouldn't, in that case, have sent Cloe the postcard. In its own fashion that postcard was a tease, like so much of what Cloe had already written. But it was a tease with faintly sinister, even desperate, overtones. There was a kind of invisible appeal in it which Cloe herself may have intuited.

Nancy had found 'this charming spot', and she sent love to her friend's fiancé – banal sentiments which with variations must have featured on any number of holiday postcards – and yet she ended by writing 'Don't forget me.' That could have been facetious too, of course; and yet I could hardly think so, no matter how discernible, if elusive, was the element of teasing. Nancy was 'living' somewhere – the word had an unmistakably solid sound about it – and although the address she gave made her perfectly accessible, she still asked not to be forgotten. Admittedly the tease element still persisted here. I had never heard of Mouriez – it must be quite a small place – but unless Nancy was very firmly dug in, and known to the French postal authorities, it was most unlikely that a communication from Cloe could have reached her. There was no mention of a *Rue*, or a hotel.

It was impossible, at least for me, to resist the conclusion that she was living with someone – a man – and then to speculate whether there could possibly be anything in her claim that she had returned to a man she had met on the trip to Holland, that she was off on 'a journey back to him'. Why then was she now in France? The whole thing seemed the merest moonshine; and yet I had become so absorbed by her, or at least by her in her tale, that I almost willed myself to believe there might be something in it.

Cloe had for some time been showing signs that she would like me to go: signs that were all too familiar from previous meetings, when I had once or twice attempted to suggest that it would have been nice to stay. I finished off my glass of South-East Australian Red, into which I had put a temperate amount of Perrier. I was driving back to the flat. Cloe must, or at least should have had, quite a choice little collection of wines, from the bottles I had brought her from time to time; but she always produced a bottle of super-market stuff on the not too frequent occasions when she gave me a meal.

There was one further thing I wanted to find out about, if I could. And this too demanded a certain delicacy, for it brought up the question of Cloe's veracity versus, as it were, Nancy's day-dreaming inventiveness. According to Nancy, Cloe had told them a story about being pursued by a tall dark man after the dance, and having to put up a fight to save what used to be called her honour. Was this story true? – because if it was then a tall dark man did exist, or had existed in some form for Cloe, if not for Nancy herself. Had Nancy appropriated Cloe's tall dark man, so to speak, and used him for the purpose of her own inventions?

But no – it appeared that no tall dark man had in fact existed, even marginally and for Cloe. She laughed a bit at my cautious query: indeed she almost giggled. She, and Charles too, had got a shade tired of Nancy's satirical atti-tude to the whole exhibition, and had determined to give her a bit of her own back. So they deliberately teased her about this man. It had been unkind, said Cloe as if penitently, after Nancy, who had been out for a solitary walk, came all damp and dishevelled into the dining-room, having walked into a puddle or been splashed by a passing barge or something. The poor girl's trousers were soaked. And Cloe turned up her beautiful eyes at me, just like a guilt-conscious Magdalen.

'So no tall dark man,' I observed.

'No,' agreed Cloe. 'Neither mine nor hers.'

I didn't entirely believe her. Indeed I had the feeling that here, if I could put my finger on it, was the fishiest part of the whole business. If she and Charles had been mocking Nancy, even in a kindly spirit, with the made-up tale of the tall dark man and Cloe's successful escape from him, then Nancy had certainly got her own back in her tale of her own love and jealousy – 'murderous jealousy' – against Cloe for stealing her tall dark policeman and all the rest of her concocted drama.

'So you didn't go absent at all?' I enquired experimentally.

'Of course not!' returned Cloe with a laugh. 'Dear old Nance made all that police station business up. As well as the stuff about my being away.'

Her eyes evaded mine, and in a second or two she got up from the table. It was a hint that she would like me to depart. I found myself continuing to sit there none the less, and to gaze thoughtfully at the face which Cloe now declined to turn in my direction.

'Of course,' she said, resting her fingers upon the table as if she were the chairman of the board about to make the final speech, 'Nancy's story may have got something in it. Otherwise she wouldn't have written it all down like that.'

I acquiesced; wondering just what elements in the tale she herself thought might be true; or at least related to truths about Nancy's recent doings, which had not yet been disclosed.

'It would be nice if you could find out what she thinks she is up to,' said Cloe, evidently determined now to wind up the evening's business. 'I'm just curious to know. That's all.'

*

I found Mouriez with the minimum of trouble. It lies more or less due north of Marseille, not far from the Rhône valley, Arles and St Rémy, and in the midst of a curious local feature called Les Alpilles, which are miniature but picturesque outcroppings of limestone rock, rising abruptly from a land-scape of olive and apricot and cypress trees. Guide books are fond of the Alpilles; so was Van Gogh. The cliffs of Les Baux are close at hand: but much of the area seems neglected and empty, left to itself like so much of France, even today. It must be bliss to live in such a big country as that, so civilised and yet with so comparatively few people. Why don't I try it some time?

That's what I thought as I disembarked at a quiet moment at Marseille airport, where all the officials and gendarmes looked beautifully dressed but half asleep. On the way out I found a kiosk with a civil and uninterested young lady in a pink uniform who made no attempt to speak English. She hired me a small car and went back to her knitting and the newspaper.

I admit that I am the sort of person who is surprised, almost incredulous, when things go well, particularly if one takes the drastic step of going on holiday abroad. There was something of a fairytale about stepping into the little Renault which a mechanic drove to the airport door, and setting off, the map beside me, on the long contours of half-empty roads, which in England would be a continuous stream of lorries. There seemed at last something foreordained about this excursion: the feeling that I only had to play the part I was playing and all would come magically right, all would be well. Always a dangerously misleading state of mind, I suppose; especially as I didn't even know what it was that I looked forward to, or hoped might happen.

It just made a change really, that traditional function of a holiday for an Englishman who likes the idea of resuming his normal habits before very long. I am in any case rather subject to ups and down: moodswings is the word I suppose. For some reason I got awfully depressed after that conversation with Cloe. I can't quite think why. It seemed to be more of a kind of sadness about Cloe, and about my role in her life, than something caused by the story of Nancy Deverell. And yet I think Nancy was at the bottom of it, and the way in which I seemed at once to have identified with Nancy as a story, rather than as a human being whom I had never met.

No doubt it was naive of me to think it could be otherwise. Nancy, after all, existed for me only through what she had written; or rather *spoken*, as it almost seemed; for I felt I could hear her voice, just as I could see her face, although I had never seen the picture of the Girl in the Red Hat, which according to Cloe only marginally resembled Nancy in any case.

I realised that was not much to go on, and I daresay that something in me would have been quite content if the expedition were to prove a complete non-starter. As I drove through the flat pebble-strewn landscape of the Crau, keeping to the east of Arles, I could already hear myself reporting regretfully to Cloe that I could find no clue whatsoever regarding Nancy's whereabouts. That 'living' might have been just another tease, after all. Nancy might have already moved on. Or perhaps she was, or had been, only staying in the neighbourhood, in which case it would have been like trying to find the needle in the haystack; for although it was late October and the holiday season had long been over for the French, there would still be enough English and American tourists around in the local towns to make the identification of any Nancy-like figure seen in the streets or cafés extremely problematic.

But if Mouriez was as small as I expected it to be, and if Nancy was actually living there, then the chances of discovering her would be reasonably good. I had asked Cloe if she had a photograph, but she said she hadn't. She had said so rather dismissively in fact. Cloe and Charles are not the sort of people who spend holidays or trips abroad taking pictures of each other, like Japanese tourists.

Nor do I if it comes to that. I like travelling with a friend, or friends, if I go abroad, but I never have a camera with me. And yet I'm always eager to be sent pictures by one of the others. Roland and Matilda in the market square, taken by Robin – that sort of thing. I love it, out of pure narcissism I suppose, rather than because it helps to recapture the time past. I have a very good photographic memory, and don't need artificial aids to recall what happened and where. But I suspect that Cloe and Charles don't take photos on principle. Being so arty, genuinely so in the case of Charles, they rather despise photography, unless it happens to be art photography. I'm the opposite. I dislike the fancy stuff but adore snaps of all kinds, the more incompetently taken the better. The spontaneity, or rather the awkwardness, of any given moment that has gone by is what appeals to me, and even moves me.

I was having these reflections while sitting in a café on the main street of Mouriez two days later. It had turned out, just as I expected, to be a small place. Also totally nondescript, the sort of straggly village that tourists drive through on their way to Les Baux or Carcassonne, somewhere that's been heard of. But the non-essentiality of Mouriez is what I liked; and I couldn't help wondering, and indeed hoping, that Nancy might have liked it or be liking it too, and for the same reason.

Normally when abroad I dislike sitting in cafés. I'm always worried about whether the waiter will see me when I want to pay the bill, or if he'll just be busy and ignore me indefinitely, as has indeed happened to me a number of times, leaving me stranded in a sort of limbo, unable to move on or resume life. The French have a song about a monsieur who is waiting for his lady-love in a café, and how she never turns up because she is awaiting him in the 'café en face'. So he waits there for ever. I suspect myself that this monsieur was just unable to secure the waiter's attention.

But being French he would probably not have that problem. It's a question of self-consciousness I suppose. I find that Matilda, say, begins to fidget, and asks if I can't get hold of the waiter; and I've sometimes ended up by going inside rather humiliatingly and asking the man behind the counter, who never seems to know what I am talking about, even though I speak perfectly good French. When he understands he refers me to the waiter, and the business starts all over again.

I thought the whole idea of being in a café was that one could sit dreamily, in a Buddha-like state of trance or meditation, but that has never happened to me. Self-consciousness I suppose, as I said.

But now, in Mouriez, it was quite different. I wasn't thinking about the waiter; I was thinking about Nancy, and the possibility of her strolling past, or even sitting down at one of the other tables. Should I recognise her at once?

For no very good reason I felt confident about that. English people abroad instantly develop a sixth sense for anyone who could be a fellow-countryman, usually affecting dismay at the sight of one. On the other hand I had formed the impression that Nancy did not look particularly English, at least in the way she conducted herself. If she wasn't alone it would be harder still to identify her; and yet I continued to feel that if I did set eyes on her something would make me aware of it.

In the meantime I was quite happy to wait. Indeed, as I sat placidly in a café without bothering about the waiter, or wandered around the village shops, I realised that I was beginning positively to enjoy being on my own in Mouriez. The place suited me. I had found without trouble a modest hotel, nearly empty of guests, where they seemed pleased to have me *en demi pension*. The sun still shone, and with barely diminished warmth, though without the *grand chaleur* of

July and August. The big leaves on the plane tree in the square were barely beginning to turn colour.

I asked myself why I had never done this sort of thing before. It was so peaceful, undemanding. It depended, of course, on the fact that I had been given a job to do: otherwise I shouldn't have been enjoying it as I was. But for the moment I could forget the job, and Cloe, and even Nancy herself, and give myself up to the pleasures of being on solitary holiday. It was a variation of the behaviour example once suggested to me by an unusually sympathetic psychiatrist. One should become conscious of what ordinary happiness consists in, he said. It's like knocking one's head for a while against a wall, and then leaving off. The leaving off period is all normal people need for happiness. I wasn't feeling at all normal at the time, I remember, and I was struck by this illustration.

In the present case, in Mouriez, it was the other way round: waiting for the moment when the wall would appear, and I would have to start knocking my head against it. For whatever Nancy was like, and however I thought I was going to behave with her (I had at the moment no idea) I knew in some way that it was going to be hard work.

That's something I've always disliked. Besides, there was a more significant point. I had, as I said, been fascinated by Nancy's story. But if I were to meet her the story would in some sense be continued, with me inside it: and although that prospect should have excited me, it didn't. I couldn't help feeling a sort of dread, on the contrary, in case the whole thing should collapse and come to pieces, turn out to be nothing at all; and Nancy, the girl I was looking for, be not like her story. Not dull necessarily, or commonplace, but simply not relevant to what had become, I suppose, an unexpected part of my own inner life.

Why was I still so sure that Nancy would turn up? I think precisely because the period of waiting was so pleasant. It was bound not to last; and the interruption or end to it could only, I unconsciously assumed, be the appearance of Nancy. Where and how would she manifest herself? Would she be alone? During that pleasant interlude I really preferred not to think about it. It did cross my mind to ring Cloe, but I have always hated the telephone, and I discarded the idea as soon as I thought of it. Let Cloe stew. But what an absurd idea! No doubt both Nancy and myself had been quite out of Cloe's mind ever since I left Heathrow. She had much more important matters to concern her.

I had been in Mouriez nearly a week. The fine weather held, but I felt no urge to be a tourist and explore the country roundabout. I walked down lanes out of the village into dry silvery olive groves. That was about as far as I got. I decided to send no postcards, least of all to Cloe. Then I felt that was a bit mean, so I set off for the Post Office and was nearly there before I remembered that in France one buys stamps at the tobacco shop. By that time I was outside the post office and just opposite the village war memorial. It was the standard job, or rather one of the four or five possible standard jobs, in a grey stone composition that looks like cement or plasticine. Gravely wounded, the *poilu* is sinking back into the arms of *La France*. His rifle, the bayonet alarmingly bent, has slipped from his hand, his helmet has fallen off and his buttoned *capote* is all awry. Very realistic, but also very sanitative and soothing.

Beside the war memorial was a wooden bench, and on it sat Nancy.

I hadn't the slightest doubt about it. There were, it is true, a number of unexpected features about this girl, or rather woman; but yes, it was Nancy.

I almost turned and fled into the post office before I remembered the proverb that in the country of the blind the one-eyed man is king. I could see her, but she couldn't possibly, in the same sense, see me. I may not have looked French, but I looked sufficiently nondescript. In any case Nancy was sitting and looking at nothing.

126

And she was wearing a red hat. Or at least a sort of reddish coloured beret. But it was not by that I knew her, nor by her face. There was nothing urchin-like about those features. It looked much older than the face I had imagined from the story. It also looked tired, vacant, submissive. Almost like the face of a French woman of a certain age, who has done the family shopping and is having a bit of a sit down on the way home.

Although she couldn't see me I could hardly just stand there, gazing at her. She might look up and round at any moment; and then, I felt, the sheer excitement and self-consciousness fizzing away in me was sure to communicate itself to her somehow or other. At the moment she was like a good dog who has been told to wait outside a shop, its lead looped over a parking meter. If it saw me gazing at it the animal would, as it were, become restive and start barking.

That was the disturbing impression I had: of an entity under control of an alien situation. Free will abandoned, she would sit there until summoned or taken elsewhere by some unknown and invisible master.

I strolled on hastily down the village street. As I walked it occurred to me all of a sudden by what homely sign I had really known this woman was Nancy, even though I hadn't at the time been conscious of the fact. She was wearing a smart pair of tweed trousers, with a dark grey herring-bone pattern. Her other clothes were vaguer, though I had been aware of a blue anorak.

I gravitated towards the side of the street, got behind a plane tree and waited a minute. Then I cautiously peeped out towards the war memorial.

The woman was gone! I hastened back, careless now whether she saw me or not, wherever she was. Could she have entered the post office? I stepped quickly through its door and looked round. Two or three elderly persons, probably collecting pensions or social benefits. No Nancy.

I spent most of the rest of the morning quartering the area, almost like the virtuous hound I had momentarily imagined the girl as being, as she sat obediently by the war memorial. Somehow I didn't expect to see her again. Nor did I; although I must have gone into every shop and bar in Mouriez. Nancy – and somehow I still knew it was Nancy – had vanished.

As I sat in a small restaurant having lunch, drinking a bottle of the local red wine and feeling pleasantly tired after the morning's exertions, I began to be aware of a mild sense of relief. Nancy had gone; the little town had swallowed her up: I could get on with my odd holiday in peace. I began to tell myself that it might not have been Nancy. Nancy might in any case just be a figment of her own imagination. Or mine. I even began to entertain the idea – grotesque as it was – that Cloe had fixed the whole thing up, written the thing herself, and sent me off as a sort of absurdly elaborate practical joke. Full of strong and flavoursome red wine I went back to my hotel for a nap.

Meditating on the matter in the evening, I found myself confronted with two contradictory factors. I had seen Nancy – I was certain of it – and yet that had made me believe less, not more, in her actual and personal existence. It was as if the present reality of Nancy removed from my heart and mind the being who become alive for me in what she had written. Because I had seen Nancy, and couldn't deny it, I had also begun to feel that she had never been in Mouriez, or anywhere else. She had become, as it were, her own delusion.

Next day I rigorously didn't look for Nancy. But I needn't have worried: there was no sign of her anyway. Nor the day after that. Three days went by in this fashion; and then I saw her again.

Remarkable how easy it is to enjoy ordinary living when you are supposed to be doing something else. I am becoming a bore to myself on this topic, but it did strike me at the time that a suitable *métier* for me would be that of security guard, keeping an eye on some celebrity who might be assassinated, but never was. The rest of life would become tranquillised, a routine just demanding enough to keep one contented.

In the course of my Mouriez routines I had often passed what I suppose was the village's only tourist attraction, and that one of a very modest sort. It was a small church or chapel, romanesque in appearance and no doubt in period, which was situated on the outskirts of the village. Passing it on my way back from the little place where I often lunched, it occurred to me to try to get in. I had never bothered before. French churches, unlike English ones, are usually open during the day, but closed between noon and four o'clock. Remembering this I was about to walk on when I saw that the door of the church was slightly ajar.

Inside it was dark and empty. A carved window high up let in some light, dazzling in the gloom below. It was very small, but the feeling was decidedly numinous. Congratulating myself on having found it open at an unusual hour when there was no one at all about, I sat down briefly at the front of the church and looked round at the smooth pale stone walls, appearing faintly phosphorescent in the light from above. Spiritual as the place was I had no wish to stay long: I was looking forward to my siesta. I got up and walked back down the aisle, receiving a slight shock at seeing that someone who must have come in after me was sitting in the darkness near the door.

As I walked past to leave, with my eye more or less averted, I saw the bottoms of the tweed trousers, with their characteristic pattern. There was no doubt who it was.

Outside the church a feeling almost of panic overtook me. It was like being stalked. Yet what could be more natural than that a woman in a French village, with a grindingly busy household day, should pause for a few moments' repose and refreshment, in a church or on a bench beside the war memorial?

Yes; but Nancy was not a village woman, nor was she

French. Was she living as if she were, and if so what was the reason? Did she now have some commitment, which made her live like that, and in a place like this one?

I was painfully conscious of the fact that I didn't really want to find out. The whole interest of this woman who was Nancy (if indeed she was Nancy) seemed to have evaporated. I felt sure that I wanted to live out my little holiday in peace and solitariness; and then go home.

None the less the brick wall that the psychologist (a humorous man for one of his profession) had spoken of, was looming unmistakably before me; and I knew the moment had come to start knocking my head against it. It was a categorical imperative: I had no choice. All I could manage by way of solace was to fix my mind on the blessed later moment when I should be able to stop doing it: that is to say, get shot of Nancy, or whoever she was, and go back to England. And yet even at that moment of resolve I was not really paying attention to why I was supposed to be here in the first place. As I realised afterwards I had at that moment no thought of my errand, nor of Cloe, waiting – notionally at least – to hear what had come of it.

So I found myself gazing feverishly up towards the roof of the chapel, as if trying to estimate, like a conscientious tourist, how its outside appearance corresponded with what I had seen inside. This time the person who was in there could hardly disappear, as she had done on the previous occasion. She would have to come out; and although I had no idea what I should do when she did, I at least waited resolutely in the empty street with the excuse, if anyone noticed me, that I was studying the architecture of the church.

In fact she came out almost at once. Although my head and eyes were in the air I was aware of it: also that she had turned back down the village street. Cautiously bringing my eyes down to ground level, I saw the blue anorak and tweed trousers receding, already thirty yards or so away. The

French nowadays tend to look like anybody else, and this woman could easily have been French, despite the rather unusual and Britannic-looking trousers – younger French women of all classes wear trousers too.

And yet I remember thinking afterwards that Nancy had contrived to seem as if she might be a local, although she continued to wear the same clothes and present the same appearance. Women are much better than men at changing the way they look without seeming to try; perhaps even without knowing that they've done so.

There was nothing for it but to walk up the street after her, telling myself that she could have no idea who I was, and that in the country of the blind the one-eyed man is king. True, I was walking after her, but in the straggly main street of Mouriez a harmless tourist could hardly avoid doing that. I imagined her coming out of church and walking straight off down the street without a glance; but if she had noticed me for a moment she could at once have seen that I was a tourist, and probably English. I don't flatter myself that my ordinary appearance had changed, just because I was in France.

And yet I was somehow sure now that she was conscious of me. Who was stalking whom? This rather disquieting thought occurred to me as I followed her in a leisurely way, with my hands in my pockets; and then it was banished by something like panic as she stopped, turned around, and stood waiting for me to come up to her. I hope my step didn't falter. In a moment I was alongside, although still pretending not to look at her, nor to appear conscious that she had stopped and was looking at me.

'You're English, aren't you?' she demanded.

I looked at her then all right. Her face was suddenly and fiercely eager, and much younger that it had looked the last time, when she had been sitting by the war memorial. Now it was the sort of face I could imagine being appropriate to a picture called 'Girl with a Red Hat'. And she was still wearing the rather grubby-looking dark red beret.

So intense was her eager avid look that I found myself almost recoiling a step. In spite of the face, and the hat, this was not at all how I had imagined Nancy. In her writing she had seemed a puckish, elfin sort of creature, capering and showing off in her own engaging way: full of her own style of fun and incapable of taking things seriously; or of having any serious things to happen to her.

It's true that Cloe didn't seem to think that: otherwise I wouldn't, I suppose, have been in Mouriez. And if there was any truth at all in Nancy's tale Cloe must have known about it, or at least something about it. I found myself wondering at that moment just what had happened that last night at the Hague, when – according to Cloe – Nancy had been frightened, and had asked her to spend the night in the room.

'Well yes, I'm a visitor,' I said, in what must have sounded a feeble rather intimidated sort of voice. I still have the advantage I thought. She doesn't know who I am and what I'm here for. She can't possibly know.

The Nancy figure looked quickly up and down the street. Even this glance somehow seemed alarmingly genuine, and not just Nancy-in-her-story, pretending to be a secret agent or something. In spite of the change between this woman and the one by the war memorial, the real difference for me was the one between Nancy Deverell as she appeared in her own story, or extended letter, and this one who wore the same trousers – a somewhat grotesque detail – but who seemed otherwise to have no connection with the girl whose fantasy about herself had intrigued me so much.

'How long are you staying here?' enquired this present Nancy. And her voice was certainly an English one.

'I'm on holiday for a few days,' I answered her, feeling flustered. 'Pottering through Provence, you know,' I went on inanely, and found myself giving a sort of giggle.

The woman took no notice but seemed to make a kind of calculation.

'Could you please meet me in the café tomorrow evening? By the square,' she went on impatiently, as I must have looked particularly clueless; and then, in a more considerate tone, 'if you're still going to be here in Mouriez.'

So far as I could remember there were at least three cafés in that area; but from what she said I had the impression that locals considered one of them to be 'the café', and I thought I knew which one she must have in mind. In any case I felt as nervous as a subordinate who is disinclined to irritate the boss with superfluous questions.

Why, if she felt lonely and wanted an English visitor to talk to, did she have to wait till tomorrow evening? Why not now, or later on today? She seemed busy and in a hurry, however, as she just said 'see you' and rushed off up the street. She hadn't mentioned a specific time, so far as I could remember, and had certainly not waited for any positive agreement on my part.

I had a lot to think about; but the chief thing I thought was that my own pleasant time off duty was coming to an end. I had certainly not acted very forcefully up to now. Why hadn't I simply gone with this woman, engaging her in conversation and refusing to be shaken off? She would have had to talk in that case; and I should certainly have got some idea of who she was, and where she was living.

Probably, I thought, because I just didn't want to find out. I even seriously considered getting into my little Renault and leaving Mouriez that afternoon. That was the effect the woman had had on me. Her whole personality, or at least the impression it made on me during our brief encounter, was upsetting.

I had no idea then why this should be so; nor did I find out when – inevitably as it seemed – I went to the café by the square the following evening. Of course I had already reconnoitred the café situation; and after patronising two of them the evening before I had no doubt which one she had in mind. Nor was I wrong.

At five o'clock, when I arrived, she was already sitting at one of the outside tables. The evening was by no means warm. A chilly breeze, although not, I'm glad to say, a *mistral*, made itself felt occasionally; and once or twice a large leaf, still green, detached itself from the massive plane tree overhead and twirled down to the pavement. Nancy was the only customer sitting outside, though a couple of boys were scuffling round the empty tables, sometimes climbing on to one of them while they shouted at each other in shrill incomprehensible tones. A young waiter, ignoring them, stood in the doorway and gazed discontentedly across the square.

What I was quite unprepared for was the way Nancy – the girl? the woman? – the Nancy at any rate of this evening – received me. Jumping up she took both my hands in hers; and then, relinquishing one of them, beckoned to the waiter, who came hastening over in a way no waiter had ever been known to do for me.

'What'll you drink?' demanded this new Nancy; and then, before I could reply, said 'I should have a Cynar. That's what I'm having.'

I acquiesced rather helplessly, and the waiter actually seemed to bow before he hurried off. In a few seconds he was back with a small brown drink, similar to the one in front of Nancy. Meanwhile she had continued to hold both my hands and smile dazzlingly into my face. If the waiter had romantic ideas about her he must have realised he wasn't going to get in on the act, at least not this evening.

Giving my hands a final squeeze she picked up her drink. 'Ciao,' she said, and knocked it back.

'Ciao' is, or was, I fancy, the kind of salutation given by the sprightly folk of Islington or Notting Hill. It had a slightly outlandish and outmoded sound to it. It seemed entirely in keeping with the Nancy I had met with in her own story.

I said 'Ciao' in a more subdued way, and took a moderate sip. It tasted like a mixture of artichokes and syrup of figs, but in an odd way was not bad, and distinctly bracing. I was aware of at least a certain amount of alcohol in it; and something like that was what I needed.

I couldn't take my eyes off this new Nancy. Although the heat of the summer was over she wore a flimsy summer dress, exposing a good deal of her arms, legs and chest, which had a touchingly white and vulnerable appearance. She was hatless, and her dark hair was neatly arranged in a sort of bob. She looked about sixteen, and as different from the woman I had seen by the chapel or the war memorial as it was possible to be.

The animation in her face was positively roguish. It gave the impression that she and I were delinquent schoolgirls, or perhaps a schoolgirl and her schoolboy friend, playing truant for the day and entering a place of refreshment that was strictly out of bounds. It made me remember the stories by Angela Brazil – *Freddie of the Lower Fifth, The Worst Girl at St Chad's* – which both my sister and I had been fond of in our own childhood. Nancy in the café breathed the same silly sense of shared adventure.

But chiefly I marvelled at the change in her, and at my own continued ignorance of what could have brought it about. This was undoubtedly the Nancy who had written that cock-and-bull tale of her adventures at the Hague. And I remembered – it was a reassuring thing to remember – that she had no idea I had read that yarn, any more than I had of what she was doing here. Or of what had brought about the change between this obviously English girl, in her blue C&A summer dress, and the almost middle-aged figure, undemonstratively resigned to the cares and toils of existence, whom I had encountered before.

I couldn't help wondering if it was I myself who had

brought about the change. It was conceited of me I know, but was it possible that the sight not just of another English person, but of me as a specific sort of English person, had caused this remarkable transformation?

The next moment Nancy herself seemed to indicate that there might be something in this idea, which naturally I couldn't help finding a rather attractive one.

'D'you know, I've been stalking you all over Mouriez!' she said flirtatiously, leaning forward over our drinks so that her mouth was close to mine. I smelled the Cynar on her breath, a syrupy nursery smell. Feeling almost light-headed I found myself grinning back at her. So I was the desired one, the fortunate fellow at whose head this extraordinary girl was, however incomprehensibly, flinging herself.

Next moment she said something much more incomprehensible. 'I had to wait for my husband.' She pursed her lips and looked away from me for a moment.

'Yes, of course,' I found myself replying, while a cold douche of water seemed to be descending on me. I shivered. The evening breeze was chilly, though I was more warmly clad than Nancy seemed to be.

With that immediate sympathy or intuition I was to come to know in the next few days she jumped up at once. 'We'll get cold sitting here,' she said. 'Let's go and have something to eat, shall we?'

She waved at the waiter, who was instantly beside her. I had noticed him taking a covert interest in us as he stood by the café door.

I fumbled rapidly in my pockets, but before I could get anywhere she had taken money from her bag and handed it with a smile to the waiter, who thanked her with emphasis. He didn't even give me a look.

It was still early to eat, and we strolled away from the main square, she with her arm through mine. Her gesture seemed quite natural, as if we were a pair of lovers so used by now to that status that we were almost absent-minded

136

about it. I found myself none the less stealing selfconscious glances at the people we passed in the street, or sitting in the cafés, as if I was expecting them all to be staring at us. Something in the oldfashioned unchanged feel I'd come to have of the village since I'd been living there, which seemed for a long time now ('Living in this charming spot', as Nancy had written on her postcard) made me remember French novels of the nineteenth century, in which a village might be scandalised by the affair between a female resident and an unknown young man from Paris, who walk shamelessly down the street together, to the scandal of the locals. Such 'provincial manners' seemed as if they might be native to the atmosphere of Mouriez, although in fact nobody seemed to be paying Nancy and me any attention at all.

'I had to wait for my husband,' Nancy had said. The phrase could easily occur in the kind of novel I had in mind. All the heroines in them had husbands, either stupid or repressive or both. What on earth it could mean in the present context was another matter. Surely it could only be part of Nancy's fantasy – an 'ongoing' fantasy, as might be said today? Something in me assumed this so completely that I found myself embarking on my own kind of day-dream, as if it might move in some sort of harmony with hers. I saw us as a pair of lovers, star-crossed by circumstances no doubt, leading a brief idyll together before life foreclosed on us and drove us apart – Nancy to her 'husband' in Mouriez, me back to my indeterminate existence in London.

And yet something sinister was involved: always had been involved, as I had obscurely perceived, in Nancy's fantasies. Perhaps it was the red hat, frequently stressed by Nancy as the emblem of adventurousness, and also of scenes that could be threatening, even fatal. The young woman certainly had a vivid imagination. I was reminded for some reason of that story, which almost everybody seemed to know in one form or another, about the man – sometimes an army officer, sometimes a mere civilian – who is invited by a mysterious woman to a rendezvous in her house, where after a delicious dinner the pair go to bed. In the most harmless version the man receives a postcard nine months later which reads 'Thankyou. It is a beautiful boy.' (The war is on, the woman's husband has been killed, and she needs a son and heir.) In other versions the man wakes up in the gutter next morning, having been drugged and castrated. Or finds afterwards that their amorous dalliance has been viewed by a bunch of voyeurs from behind curtains in the bedroom; and that he has been an unknowing participant in a specialist brothel.

I suppose the point is that everyone who knows this story goes for some particular variation of it. Nowadays, our instincts are no doubt conditioned by books and the media to prefer the most violent and gruesome version. That's only to be expected. What about Nancy's own fantasies in this light? In some ways she couldn't fail to seem to me a straightforward and even a sensible young woman, as well as quite a humorous one. That was the impression that came from behind the story she had written down, and also from our meeting of this evening, bizarre as her style of behaviour might seem to be. In my own instinctive and probably irrational way I felt that only a girl who was basically sensible could indulge herself in daydreams of that kind. Or to put it the other way round, that such a lively imaginative life must naturally be kept cordoned off by its owner from a basically sensible and rational style of existence.

In the rapid way they occur I intertwined such thoughts as we strolled down the village street, with her arm through mine. She asked how I liked Mouriez, but was quite incurious about how I had come to be there. It was an excitement for me – almost part of my own fantasy you might say – to know that I was concealing my own prior knowledge of her, and that I definitely proposed to go on doing so. It seemed natural not to ask her any questions about herself; and of course there was, in a sense, no need for me to do so. There was a freedom about this, as there is about most casual holiday contacts, when two people seem to click, for the time being and in a given set of circumstances.

At the end of the street she paused, as if for reflection, and I was vividly reminded of the occasion in her story when she walks the streets of the Hague with Charles and Cloe in search of somewhere to dine. I hoped that no establishment resembling the Israeli restaurant existed in Mouriez. But to my surprise she turned to me, as if after pondering the matter for a moment or two, and asked if I knew of anywhere agreeable to eat. I suggested one of the places I had found for myself, and found most sympathetic; and as we retraced our steps towards it I wondered why, if she had been 'living' in Mouriez, she knew so little about its amenities. She must have been 'living' very quietly; but how, and where?

By the end of our meal she had wholly recovered the practical ascendancy over me that she had shown in the café. She summoned the waiter and paid the bill. All my protests were unavailing. Nor did she seem to care in the least that the waiter – a good-looking young man who gave the impression he was really an architect or something and was just earning some extra francs – gave us an amused look, as if aware that she had picked me up. If he were interested, which he probably wasn't, he must have been surprised by what she did next: for she told me to meet her at the café the following evening, stood up, and was out of the restaurant and gone in a flash. I was left sitting in front of the large cognac which she had ordered me, against my protests.

Perhaps the waiter was a bit interested, for he turned up his eyes and gave me a commiserating look as he came to the table to pick up the large tip she had left. By that time I too was on my way out, abandoning the cognac. *'Ah, les femmes'*, the waiter seemed to say, but no doubt I was merely imagining such an oldfashioned reaction.

Nancy had of course disappeared, and I was quite certain it would be no good trying to look for her. She had given me her instructions before vanishing, and I would meet her at the same place the next evening. So much was certain. But it was equally certain that during the evening I had failed to find out anything about her at all: where she was living, what she was doing. As for the 'husband' she had to 'wait for', no more had been said about him. Why hadn't I enquired further, with discretion naturally, and by indirections? I can only say that there seemed to be no point in it. Nancy, I was sure, was merely setting up the scene for one of her fantasies, like a painter preparing a canvas. I was, in one sense, to be the model or sitter: that is to say the person privileged to receive a new set of impressions about herself, and for the benefit of herself.

Although I felt quite confident about that I had to admit that I was at a loss when it came to explaining the difference between Nancy as I had first seen her, and the Nancy who had appeared at the café this evening. But on further reflection it was obvious enough. Nancy had been waiting for someone to operate on, or rather at. The sprightly girl of tonight, in the blue dress, had been the butterfly waiting to emerge from the chrysalis. She had gaily admitted tonight to having reconnoitred me, stalking me over a period of days before she had made her move. What she had been waiting for had been someone like myself, a visitor from her own country, on whom she could practise being her chosen self, the Nancy of the tale she had defiantly sent her friend Cloe. Before then she had been living in Mouriez like a spider in the corner of its web, drawing no attention to herself. Even the shapeless reddish beret she had been wearing was – I had seen others not unlike it in Mouriez – a badge of middle-aged and parochial orthodoxy. She could hardly have passed as a Frenchwoman, but she could at least have dispelled any local curiosity by superficially resembling one.

So I reasoned as I lay in bed, thinking over the events of

the evening. It was natural she should have been determined, at least for this occasion, to pay her own way. A tourist, however goodnatured and gullible, might well have become suspicious of acquaintance with a local lady who expected him to pick up the bill on every occasion. But I had a twinge of discomfort, even jealousy, as I thought of her spending the summer here – 'living' here as she had put it on the postcard – when the place must have been if not swarming with tourists, then at least frequented by English visitors with whom she could have struck up temporary acquaintance, as she had done with me. Perhaps I had not been the first?

I found myself almost wishing that she knew who I was – a friend of Cloe's – and had been looking forward to meeting me; but of course there was no possibility of that; and I could only take comfort from knowing so much about her, at least about her inner self, while she knew nothing of me. And yet, so quickly did our intimacy seem to grow, I already began to have the feeling the next evening that she had known me, as well as I her, for ages.

That was the magical thing about it. At the end of the next evening I remained, after she had abruptly left as she had done the night before, in a state of that helpless euphoria one experiences after falling in love. It is usually a fairly brief experience, because anxieties of various kinds are apt to take over almost at once, but it's bliss while it lasts.

Miraculously, in my case, as I soon became aware, there were no anxieties. Why should there have been? I was fascinated by Nancy; I was even infatuated by something about her; and yet it wasn't love exactly. I had not the smallest desire to declare myself, to take her in my arms and kiss her, still less to go to bed with her; and I could tell, indeed I could be quite sure, that she had no such feelings about me. Instead I was extremely aware of the fact that she was waiting for the moment, not when love should be declared or anything of that sort, but when she would start telling me about herself:

141

and telling me about herself, for Nancy, would certainly be making up stories about herself. I longed to hear them.

I didn't have to wait long. After three or four days of our meetings, always in the evening and always abruptly terminated, she asked if I had a car. Up to then we had chatted easily about all sorts of things; communication was never in the least a problem. She had told me she was living here because it was convenient for Arles and St Remy and Tarascon, biggish places in which she would prefer not to be resident, and yet places that appealed because of their association with art. She hoped to be a painter, or at least to paint pictures. 'Unlikely pictures' as she put it, which would recall Van Gogh and Provence and all that while being quite different from it; which would surprise by discovering small, unlovely nooks and corners – factory farm buildings, store-houses, ditches, derelict sheds – which painting might turn into something special.

I admit I paid very little attention to this sort of thing coming from Nancy. The painting business was just a pose: and a pose is a very different thing from a story about yourself. I was waiting for her story, and when she asked me about the car I felt for some reason that the story could not be far off. Our relations must be about to enter a new phase. Nor was I wrong.

And yet by the time it happened I hardly cared. I was besotted with Nancy as a phenomenon: the genuineness of which – for me at least – was unmistakable. Any stories she told me could only be synthetic or obviously false compared to the being who seemed to have revealed herself to me here in Mouriez as the true Nancy.

That was no doubt the egoism that comes with love – indeed habitually replaces it, after the first revelation. Now I only wanted my own Nancy. The thought of all the other relationships and contacts which she must have – quite apart from the tales she made up for herself and about herself – were repellent to me. I didn't want to be told about them.

And she did not tell me. The first evening, after we got to the restaurant, she had simply said, like the schoolgirl she then appeared to me to be, 'I'm Nancy. What's your name please?' Most people seem interested, perhaps out of politeness, when they hear my Christian name, but Nancy made no comment when I said 'Roland', and so far as I can remember my name hardly afterwards passed her lips. I think she never wanted to know who I was.

Which was fair enough, as in a sense I had soon begun not to want to know who she was either. I revelled in her: indeed we revelled in each other, because there was no question of getting to know one another. Very relaxing.

We chattered away in English together like a pair of magpies, attracting glances of mild Gallic disapproval from our fellow clients in café or restaurant. The French may speak Franglais and have become Europeanised, but their aesthetic distaste for the manners and behaviour of other nations is never far below the surface.

After that first moment when she had seized both my hands Nancy never touched me. Nor I her. I think neither of us felt the slightest wish to.

Nevertheless I was extremely aware of Nancy's physical presence as she sat beside me in the car a few days later. To be blunt, she smelt: and I don't mean of perfume and that sort of thing. She was still wearing the flimsy blue dress she had had on in the café, and I don't think it had been washed for some time, or her underclothes either. The sun was really hot that day, beating down on the roof of the car. I had opened the window, but Nancy said, 'Oh, it blows me about so much,' and asked me to close it. Then we were really hot: I had taken my coat off.

Nancy's thin legs sprawled out inelegantly in front of her; and with her funny little face and pageboy bob, as I thought of it, she really did look like a twelve-year-old who has not yet begun to shave, dressed up by his sister. That displeased me, I must own: it was no part of my Nancy; but I was

143

already aware that with this Protean being 'my own Nancy' was not likely to stay with me for long. Transformations would always be taking place. Besides I hardly knew myself what my own Nancy was, or was like. I had just given myself up to her, and to the ease we seemed to feel together.

In the car that ease took the form of silence: just as in the restaurant or café it had taken the form of chatter, laughter, continual interruptions of each other. I began, as I drove, to have my own daydream, actually too crude to be called even a daydream. I thought of Cloe, with her rounded form, her well-filled legs, all the self-possessed elegance which I habitually and vainly desired. Why couldn't Cloe be like Nancy? – a creature I could be as wholly at ease with as I was with Nancy now, and yet a creature whom I ardently wanted? Never the place, the time, and the girl altogether, as the poet says; but he might have added that in any case it would never be the right girl at the right moment, for the right purpose. For had Cloe been beside me now I should have been consumed with anxieties – where should we go? where stop for lunch? would she enjoy it? – anxieties that would have almost displaced my desire for that one thing only, as people used to say. Indeed 'the one thing only' would have constituted the biggest, most overwhelming anxiety of all.

And now I felt no anxieties of any kind. Sitting peacefully beside Nancy, inhaling her remarkable odour, seeing those unattractive legs sprawling into scuffed espadrilles, I didn't care what happened. It was the happiest sensation. I knew we should soon start talking again, communing together …. She would be laughing, chuckling into my face, breaking off to become companionably abstracted for a moment. French roads are still admirably suited to driving along in a dream: best of all a dream that has no need or wish for fulfilment.

I'd already noticed Nancy's gift for knowing what I was thinking, and it disturbed me not at all. On the contrary. It was the only kind of interest she seemed to take in me, and in a subtle way a very flattering one. Now she said quite suddenly, and with her usual giggly laugh: 'You're noticing the way I smell, aren't you? It's my husband's fault. He tells me not to wash. He prefers me that way.'

I answered something I suppose, but I don't know what. The road was straight and empty and I turned my head to look at her. Her eyes were sparkling with pleasure but they were friendly too, even kindly. She was enjoying herself, but she wanted me to do the same.

My first thought, and it seemed likely to be a correct one, was that she had suggested the car trip in order to have a good context for starting to make up things about herself. Things for my benefit, and no doubt for hers. Like a railway carriage, the car made the right sort of milieu for her to enter upon her fantasies, as if obliquely. Notwithstanding all that I felt strangely discomposed. There is a moment in *Othello*, a play I used to have to teach at the college, when Iago decides to give his master some graphic indication of Desdemona's guilt with Cassio. He says he saw Cassio wipe his beard with Desdemona's handkerchief, which she must have given him. The intimacy implied by this is somehow revolting: no wonder it drives Othello mad.

Although I knew she must be making it up, this sudden glimpse behind the curtain of an imagined matrimonial intimacy was none the less disturbing. It was the second time Nancy had mentioned her 'husband'; and I could not help feeling that my lack of apparent response to that first reference had caused her now to try deliberately to shock me. If so she had succeeded. When a wife refers in public to 'my husband', it is usually in a colourless though mildly possessive and even smug tone, as if specifying some area of her life which has, so to speak, been satisfactorily dealt with. No indication of the man is given, beyond this formal and theoretic function. But now Nancy had chosen to impart a detail of married life, however hypothetical it must be in her case, which could hardly fail to disconcert and even embar-

145

rass whatever man she might be talking to. Men recognise each other's sexual oddities, after all, even if they do not share them.

After recovering from the momentary shock I determined not to let the moment pass. If Nancy was trying to lead me on I would press forward deliberately. Previously it had been part of the fun of knowing her not to ask any questions. Now it seemed imperative to do so if our relationship was in any sense to be maintained.

'Please, Nancy,' I began, 'don't be so mysterious. Who is this husband of yours? Is he in Mouriez? Why can't I meet him?'

I tried to speak lightly but quite seriously, as if I didn't disbelieve for a moment that there was such a person, but that up to now Nancy herself had chosen that he, her husband, should play no part whatever in our relationship.

'No, you can't meet him,' the girl teased on in her amiable way, 'because he's in Jerusalem.'

This was really a bit much, but I wasn't going to let her get away with it. If she thought she could put me out of countenance by mocking me I would show her she was wrong. I saw at once that she was joining up the fantasies about herself she was now going to tell me, with the ones she had invented in her letter to Cloe. She didn't know that I knew about those, and of course I wasn't going to reveal that I did. But that didn't mean I couldn't tease her back, and simulate the incredulity that I naturally felt.

'He flies to Jerusalem from Marseille,' she added in a matter-of-fact tone. 'Usually via Rome.'

'OK, pull the other one,' I told her, turning my head again to smile at her in the affectionate bantering way that had developed so swiftly and so pleasantly between us in the few days we had known each other. 'You told me at the café when we first met that you'd had to wait for him before you could come out. I assumed he'd come home, and was minding the baby.'

146

I gave the tease back in spades with these last words; but I managed to do so, I hope, in Nancy's own friendly manner.

But she trumped my move by becoming immediately serious. 'There's no baby yet,' she said, and she sounded quite portentous. 'We're waiting until he gets the office job he's put in for.'

'Then what's he doing now?'

'He works under cover.'

Nancy contrived to say this with a slight air of constraint. She wasn't reproaching me for my curiosity, but giving the merest hint of warning that she wouldn't be prepared to discuss this matter much further, or in any detail.

It was superbly done; and in my admiration I almost cried out, 'Bravo.' This was the true story of her own story, and as I drove along I felt quite lost in admiration. Our silence had again become companionable, and I did not feel inclined to break it. Nancy's present romance for my benefit was soundly based on the untidy plausibility of real things and events. When she had told me she had had to wait for her husband the information was only ambiguous in the sense that all perfunctory comments about private life are. She might have meant – indeed from her own point of view she obviously did mean – that she had seen me in Mouriez, an English tourist who might be a promising source of gossip and chat in her French exile; but that it was better to wait until her husband had set off for Marseille or somewhere, *en route* for wherever it was he was going. Jerusalem, apparently.

I felt now that honour was satisfied; and that there was no need for further investigation into Nancy's current imaginary world, or perhaps I should say the world of her imagination. She had her own right to it after all. If she wanted to amuse herself by making up more tales to tell me, that was her affair.

I had a vulgar temptation to remark, deadpan, that with her husband away there was no reason why she shouldn't take a shower or two, and even wash her clothes. But of course I wouldn't yield to it. Nancy's hygienic arrangements, or rather the lack of them, were her own concern. I did find myself reflecting, none the less, that there was no indication in her 'letter' to Cloe that she liked being a dirty girl – or a dirty boygirl, as she herself might then have put it. What had made her so? – and what, come to that, had in sober fact brought her to Mouriez? There must, as people say, have been something. But having tacitly accepted Nancy's proffered fantasy I couldn't very well enquire too closely into what I considered her 'real' situation. I confined myself, a few minutes later, to some mild query about whether she had any relatives living in France. She said she formerly had – a mother now dead – but her mother's relations by marriage lived in the north or in Paris, and she hardly ever saw them.

This was true, or at least agreed with what Cloe had told me; and I realised that nuggets of truth were bound to lie embedded in any yarn that the girl might feel inclined to make up about her goings-on. Cloe herself had hinted as much when she asked me what I thought about Nancy's writings. Nancy, for one thing, must be *living* somewhere in Mouriez. By herself? How could I know? If I asked she would only tell me another tall tale. Here I was, feeling closer to her at every encounter, and yet she seemed as far away as ever: further, if anything.

By this time we were approaching Tarascon, the birthplace, as I now recalled, of another teller of tall tales. I wondered if Nancy had heard of Alphonse Daudet's once well-known creation, Tartarin. Could there be some connection between the place where she was living, and the mercurial Provençal who improved the story of his life to amaze his compatriots? But that seemed too fanciful; or at least Nanciful. She was asking me now if I wanted to see the castle. I said I thought not, unless she was keen. I am allergic to the picturesque, although the great bulk of the place, as we drove helplessly past it in the traffic stream, was certainly impressive. But it was a relief to be swept onwards, across the Rhône. Parking is just as impossible in French towns as in English ones, and can be even harder on the nerves.

'Pont du Gard!' chortled Nancy suddenly. 'That's the place. You can sound your horn there.'

The way she uttered the suggestion, teasing the associations of my name but not mentioning it, made me feel a little sour. Truth to tell, I was beginning to weary a bit of the drive, and even of her company. The atmosphere inside the car and the unseasonal heat (although autumn can be as hot as summer in that part of the world) combined to make me long to be back in the quiet streets of Mouriez, before I met her. 'He works undercover' indeed! I thought disgustedly of all the rubbish she had written down about her policeman, or porter, and her fantasy about being strangled by him. Now that I had found Nancy, was there any point in pursuing the acquaintance? I felt a growing determination to lay my cards on the table, even to reveal that I had been sent out by Cloe to see if she were 'all right': to ask point blank how she was living, and if anyone else was involved. It was really too provoking to be played around with in this manner by the tiring girl, intrigued and fascinated as I had become by her; and however much I now felt at home with her when we met in our own odd way.

As usual, Nancy seemed to sense at once what I was feeling and thinking; and for the first time her evident awareness made me feel spied upon, even hunted and trapped. I didn't turn to look at her as she started speaking.

'I know you're wondering what I'm doing here,' she started off in a coaxing tone. 'It must seem odd for a married woman to pick you up like that and expect you to keep her company. But I knew I should feel terribly lonely when Putzi had to go away' – her voice shook, dwindling into that of a little girl, and she seemed near to tears – 'and I was so frightened of being on my own, or at least having nobody

149

here that I knew; and I couldn't help clutching at the chance of having someone to talk to; and you've been wonderful to me; and what a bit of luck it was for me to have found you.'

She uttered this breathlessly, and she put a hand out somewhere near my knee; but she didn't touch me.

I should have been moved by this, and indeed I was mollified; but any emotion inside me could only have been a response to her 'story', not to herself. If she told me the truth, humbly admitting that she had told me, and Cloe too incidentally, a pack of lies; and that now she really needed my help and support, even my escort back to England – why, that would be another matter. I wouldn't have liked it, but that would at least be that. As it was I felt I had got enough 'story' of my own now, from my acquaintance with Nancy and with Mouriez; and it was time to change all that, and make our relationship, which had become so easy and as it were so hopeful, one of real trust. I was genuinely beginning to think that Nancy *was* in trouble of some sort, possibly some kind of entanglement with a young Frenchman, which he, or she, was now regretting and wanting to escape from. It could well be pitifully commonplace, even sordid; but it would be a relief to hear about it, and to believe in it, after all the lies she had told.

I determined to be ruthless, and to press her on this 'Putzi' business, the imaginary husband whose duties had called him to Jerusalem. It looked as if he might just as well have been called Haroun al Raschid, and have come out of the Arabian Nights.

'I hope your husband won't object to your consorting with me while he's away,' I remarked with heavy irony. 'Even though we only meet respectably in cafés, and I've no idea even where you live.'

'Oh no, he wouldn't mind at all,' she said earnestly, and as if humbly. She seemed to find reassurance in the thought of her husband's tolerance and good nature. 'I've often worked for him ....' For a moment she sounded eager, as if she wanted to go on, and then she stopped herself, as if suddenly remembering that she mustn't give anything away.

'Worked where?' I pressed her.

'Oh, different places. We were married in Jerusalem.'

'And where were you before that?'

'Oh, all over the place,' she said impatiently. 'Beirut once. Frankfurt ....' She began even more to sound as if she'd had enough of this, and was remembering, rather late in the day, the duty of discretion.

'Ever in Holland? At the Hague or Amsterdam?'

'No.'

'I only asked because that's the kind of place where innocent folk like myself imagine lots of espionage in progress, as well as drug-smuggling and all that sort of thing.'

I spoke quite admiringly, as if I accepted without question her account of what she had done, but was disclaiming any ability, on my own account, to enter into such an arcane world.

Stealing a glance at her I could see she was reassured by my tone.

'My husband's very much against drugs,' she said in a voice of virtue, as if on his behalf. 'But I'd rather not talk about what he does. I can only tell you it's for the benefit of his country. And, indirectly, of all countries.'

She had won again: that was clear. What could one say in the face of this pretence to a kind of universal uprightness? Nancy's little face looked quite grave, as if she were in church, the old kind of church before these happy-clappy days. But I felt that I still had a card or two in my hand.

'I promise not to make any more tiresome enquiries,' I told her. 'I've got so fond of you, Nancy, if you don't mind my saying so, that I don't want to bother you in any way about your private life, your real life ....' I stumbled deliberately over the words. 'It was such a piece of luck meeting you when I'm all on my own. It's the sort of thing every solitary tourist longs to happen, and it never does. Such a stroke of luck that you happened to pop into the St Pierre chapel (I had found out the name) when I was studying it. I'd promised myself to make a study of all those little Romanesque places in Provence – got a contract for a book as a matter of fact. But they can wait. I've got plenty of time. I'm a gentleman of leisure. And I'd far rather wander about the country with you, so long as you'll let me.'

It was the longest consecutive speech I'd ever made to her, and to me it sounded totally unconvincing. I only hoped it didn't sound the same to her. Making things up did give me a thrill, I own; and I thought I could see, on a very modest level, why Nancy and people like her concocted such tall stories about themselves. It had occurred to me while I was as it were 'grilling' Nancy, however lightly, that she, in her role as an undercover agent's wife, might feel she ought to show suspicion of a man she had come in contact with, as she had with me. In a sense she had done so, and I had made, I felt, the correct move in response. I wondered briefly whether people who romanced on Nancy's scale were better or worse at detecting the same sort of story made up by someone else. Even though mine was a much more modest one.

I rather liked the idea of the young man I had so glibly concocted for her benefit. But the idea of him – freshly sprung from the head as he was – put me in mind of something else that I had occasionally considered in the last few days. Could Nancy be making, in her own peculiar way, a pass at me?

If I felt modest as an extempore liar about my life and activities, and I certainly did so, it was nothing to my modesty about my own charms in relation to her. Yet I could see she was lonely, and at the back of the loneliness was there not something more disquieting: a kind of desperation or wretchedness? Were her stories really intended to win her someone's love: even that of someone like myself?

I had already wondered whether her 'letter' wasn't a sort of attempt to flirt with Charles, through Cloe. Or even with Cloe herself. Nancy, it seemed to me from her story, certainly took a sort of refuge in enjoyment of her self-chosen role as a Girl in a Red Hat. Although I had never seen the picture I was beginning to realise what it must have come to mean to her. If and when I did see it I felt I should see not that it looked like Nancy, but that it was the portrait of a girl who might cause almost anything to happen to her, at any time.

I took a calculated risk. 'I know that you came to Mouriez for art's sake in a way,' I joked. 'And what a nice place to choose so that you can do your own thing, and welcome your husband home when he's been off on some assignment' – I said the last word a bit tentatively – 'and you can settle down again together.'

To my dismay there was an ominous silence. Previous silences in the car had been, as I said, entirely relaxed and comradely.

Slightly panicked I none the less ploughed on, asking her amongst other things whether she had ever seen the Vermeer collections in the Dutch museums, which surely made such an interesting contrast with Van Gogh as a later Dutch painter? Those yellow chairs and sunflowers and cypresses .... Did they not have their own kind of equivalent in Vermeer's interiors? I had once myself thought of trying to write something about this subject, but of course I never got started.

Perhaps it wasn't so much what I said, but the fact that it was so different from our normal carefree mode of communication. Nancy must have heard at least the tension and the artificiality in my words. None the less I babbled on.

'Oh shut up.' She got it out suddenly in a harsh creaky voice, as if she were being half strangled. Then she gave a great sob. I drove on feeling frozen.

'What's come over you?' She sounded now incredulous

rather than hurt, as if she had suddenly glimpsed what a terrible, but above all what a depressing place, the real world must be: and as if she could scarcely believe it.

'Of course you don't believe a word I've been saying about myself, do you?'

It was like a ringing challenge. Never taken up, because at that moment the Pont du Gard abruptly burst on us: the colossal beetling viaduct of golden stone, looking exactly as if the Romans must have invented railway trains – cars too – as well as so many other important things.

I braked instinctively and stopped. Nancy leapt out of the car.

'I'm going to walk across the top,' she yelled back at me.

Young people, and not so young ones too, always feel they must walk together across the top arches of the Pont du Gard. There's nothing really dangerous about it. Unless you happened not only to get giddy and slip and fall, but then to roll sideways. The flat expanse of stone is eight feet or more wide. Down the centre runs the narrow channel, once lead-lined, which gave the whole massive enterprise its point. It was not just a bridge but an aqueduct, bringing water to a prosperous and growing provincial town. (The guidebook will give you all these facts, and many others.)

It was just that I have no head for heights. The Pont du Gard is extremely high, and looks even higher when your car is parked beside the river, down below.

Nancy was already off at a run up the steep escarpment. I hung about by the car and watched her tiny silhouette appear at the top and begin to stride across. She really did look very small, her smallness indicating the span of the arches below her and the bulk of each fitted stone. She disappeared from sight towards the end of the bridge and then came into view again, strolling back jauntily. I wondered whether to wave: she showed no sign of doing so; and I hesitated from a fear – quite pointless obviously – that it might cause her to trip or stumble. Late in the year as it was, there was no other

154

visitor or tourist up there on top, although there was traffic across the bridge as usual, far beneath it.

At last, as she was nearly across and I was straining my eyes to keep her in view, she did wave, quite unmistakably. I don't think she saw me wave back: the car and I must be in shadow from where she was, and the background had become dark. But her gesture, from far away up high there, seemed to carry an immense significance. I felt suddenly and at once that I loved her: needed her, wanted to protect her. She was so far away, and in the last few days we seemed to have come so close.

All an impulse of the moment of course. By the time she was back beside me at the car I felt quite normal again, insofar as there was any kind of normality in those increasingly strange and self-perplexing days. She said nothing more about her sudden outburst of anger, nor did I. We drove off into Nîmes, and our lunch was not a success: she chose a place that turned out to be pretentious and expensive. As usual she insisted on paying: I had quite given up on that one. It was a relief to get back to home as it seemed, to Mouriez. After sitting in the café we went, without appetite in my case, to our usual place to eat, but for once we seemed to have nothing to say to each other. What Nancy had said to me in the car, and I felt I could remember every word, seemed to lie heavily between us. After she had paid and shot out into the night I ordered myself another brandy, but that did me no good at all. My bed in the hotel seemed the only proper refuge.

Waking early in the morning I found myself seriously considering going straight back to London. There was no reason why I shouldn't drive to Marseille and catch the first flight on which I could get a booking. Nancy in the evening would find me gone, or at least not there. I toyed, too, with the idea of reporting to Cloe, when I got back home, that I could find no trace of Nancy at all in Mouriez. By doing that

I would have extinguished her, got her right out of my system, if not out of my memory.

So of course when I got up I did nothing. Except potter about the streets and shops of Mouriez in the usual way. I must have been becoming quite a familiar figure there, but nobody in the shops or anywhere else showed any sign of recognising my existence, any more than they had done so when the pair of us – Nancy and I – had strolled together up the street, the first time we had properly met. So much for the chumminess, and so forth, of local village communities. But what a relief it was that no one did pay any attention to me; and that I remained, at least to myself, the one-eyed man in the country of the blind.

I was feeling like this when I saw Nancy. It was the first time I'd seen her this way since the moment in the chapel. She was not stalking me now – that was clear. She was gazing vacantly into a shop window. I was able to step quickly into another shop and take a look out after a moment to see which way she would go. Fortunately it was away from me. I let her get nearly out of sight and then followed her. Very cautiously.

Of course I had given a lot of thought to the question of where Nancy was living, and how I could find out. But it was quite impossible, after our evening meetings, to do anything about it, and would somehow have seemed ungentlemanly too. I couldn't have imposed myself on her as we left the restaurant, and if I had tried to follow her then she would have known at once. I was touched by the vacant melancholy of her appearance, so much in contrast with the animations of the day before, disquieting to me as many of these had been. Now she looked like someone who has finished with life, and who is killing time while waiting to go. Did I mean that she was no longer bothering – for that was the impression she made – to invent her stories, and so to live them?

Keeping discreetly at a distance I followed her down the

street to a point where single houses, mostly rather dilapidated, took over. Nancy turned left, and as I reached the corner and looked cautiously round I saw her letting herself in to one of the smallest and meanest of these houses. So I knew now where she lived. 'I am living here at the moment' the postcard had said, or something like that. Like everything she'd written it had a defiant or at least a deliberately jaunty sound, as if there were something she wanted both to claim and to conceal.

Whichever it was, the nondescript unkempt little place, ugly as only modern French houses on the outskirts of an old village can be, seemed all too suitable a spot for daydreams to come to an end. What could Nancy invent there? As I pondered the question a woman came out of the front door through which Nancy had disappeared. She was just an ordinary rather tough-looking French woman, neat but battered in appearance, the sort that Nancy herself had given the impression of becoming when I first saw her sitting with that patient downtrodden look by the war memorial. The woman passed me and went on towards the shops.

The likeliest thing, I concluded, was that Nancy had taken a room during the summer in that needy little establishment, and stayed on. The nearest house to me had a sun-curled notice with *Chambre à louer* in the window. That was how it must be, and the only uncertainty I still felt was about Nancy's true situation: whether there might be a real young man, or a middle-aged or even elderly one come to that, who might be the real reason for her staying on in Mouriez. Or a woman? Nancy was the kind of girl whose boyish appearance might well appeal to a certain type of Frenchwoman. Perhaps the very woman whom I had just seen coming out of the house?

It was a beautiful day, but a feeling of emptiness and depression came over me. I was no longer finding Mouriez a pleasant place to be in. How was I to fill the time before the evening meeting with Nancy, to which I was now not looking forward? The whole business had gone on long enough. Thinking distastefully of the nonsense Nancy had invented in the car about her husband, known to her as 'Putzi', her marriage in Jerusalem, all the rest of the farrago, I remembered with similar revulsion my own wonderings about whether I could be falling a bit in love with the girl; or whether she in her own bizarre way might not be making a sort of pass at me. It was true I had never loved her in the sense of desiring her – and I thought for a moment almost wistfully of Cloe back in London – but in the first few days of our acquaintance in Mouriez Nancy had certainly occupied all my thoughts and attention: all my capacity for feeling as it seemed.

The only thing I could think of to do was to go back to my hotel room, a narrow little box of which I was in any case beginning to get tired, and write down this new change that had come over the business -the unfinished business – of trying to find out about Nancy. I wasn't getting very far: nor did there seem much to find out. Nor, come to that, did I greatly care for what little there seemed to be.

To cheer myself up, since I felt really dejected, and to get the nasty little house where Nancy was living out of my mind, I stopped at the big café. Although the sun was bright on the outside tables, most of which still had their green and white umbrellas over them, I sought the dark interior, sat in a comfortable corner and ordered a Cynar. It was Nancy's drink, and I felt I owed it to her to have one more, although usually when we had sat at the café together I'd drunk a glass of white wine or a Ricard. Now as I sipped the stuff I made up my mind quite firmly to go back to England the next day.

Feeling much more cheerful after this decision, even happy, I strolled back to the hotel. It was a simple place, and there was usually no one at the reception counter, though voices were sometimes to be heard from the office place behind it. I had my key in my pocket and was just about to go upstairs when the Madame came out of the office and said she had a letter for me, just arrived. My first thought was that it must be from Cloe, bossily demanding to know how the enquiry was going; and then I remembered that Cloe did not have my address in Mouriez, even if she had wanted to write, which was itself most unlikely.

I took the envelope mechanically, and was aware that the old sourpuss was smiling at me over her moustache (carefully depilated, but still somehow a ghostly presence on her upper lip) in what seemed quite an arch way.

'Your fiancée has just been here, Monsieur', she said.

I smiled back at her. There seemed no need for understanding. The old dear had just got things wrong in some way. Among the few guests there was a dapper young man staying there, probably a commercial traveller, with whom I exchanged courtesies when we met in the upstairs corridor. All French *femmes bourgeoises* of a certain age like to see young men trapped and incarcerated in traditional ways.

'She will be staying the night with you she told me,' the woman went on. 'And you are returning to London tomorrow. She has just arrived, herself, from Paris.'

Madame positively beamed. At this time of the year she did not mind losing the odd tourist customer, like me, who had been a valueless unsocial sort of person, and English as well. But in her eyes I was at least going out in a blaze of glory, with a fiancée unexpectedly arrived from Paris.

I excused myself and went up the stairs, aware of an increasing stupefaction and indeed alarm. I still felt that some mistake must have been made, but if it hadn't what on earth could all this be about?

I tore open the envelope, which indeed had my name on it in Nancy's hand. I could be sure, for I still had the postcard she had sent to Cloe.

Dear Roland,

Such bliss such joy I can hardly begin to tell you! And as you've clearly never believed a word of what I have told you, you naff person, you won't understand anyway. But the point is I'm free! Free as the birds, free as the bird with the red feathers! But you won't understand that either – I keep forgetting. So I'm coming to you tonight at the hotel, just to stay, and flying back with you to England tomorrow, and if you don't like it you can lump it. Don't worry – I'll be sharing your bed – I suppose you're in a *matrimoniale*? – most of those little hotel French bedrooms are – but there's no necessity for you to do anything. I'm much too happy as I am. Free.

I thought you'd probably be out so I've written this. I'll see you in the café at six tonight. I haven't got much with me. Now don't go getting all mopey about it. It's not as if you have to do anything, as I said. Just take me home. Bye. Nancy.

PS Sorry to be disrupting your holiday and all that – but you must have had enough of beastly old Mouriez by now surely.

She was right about that. I *had* seen enough of beastly old Mouriez. And of Nancy too. A naff person I might be (what a disgusting phrase, though it reminded me a little of Nancy's sprightly style, in the great screed which turned out to have been aimed at Cloe) but in that case I was a naff person who could make up his mind, and quickly too.

I had till six tonight. But I must get out at once, as soon as I could. First I must fetch the car; and then pack my small bag, and pay the bill. Reasoning feverishly with myself I saw how I could shirk telling Madame. I'd tell her I'd like to settle up right away, and add a swingeing tip. Then I'd tell her we'd be back this evening. Leaving for Marseille at cockcrow – *extrêmement de bonne heure*. Early flight. Going to confirm it now.

I was packed by now, mouthing these words to myself as I worked. I hurried downstairs: no Madame of course: I rapped at the office door. She came out offendedly, wiping her mouth. Coffee, or more likely *tisane*. A smile again as I put large numbers of francs, most of what I had left, on the counter. 'Oh but monsieur, no necessity. Tonight. Or in the morning. I rise always early.'

I insist with a lot of flannelling. I put down the tip. She melts. '*A ce soir*,' and I am out of the door, trying to make my bag not too visible, and off *à grand pas* towards the square, where the little Renault is permanently parked.

I am almost there, almost at the car door, when I hear a shout behind me. 'Roland! Roland!'

I don't know why I should be writing this now in the historic present. It's true that, for me, I was pretty tensed up at the time, and things seemed to go, or come, from moment to moment with great urgency. The violence of my desire to get away surprised me at the time and still surprises me now: even though impressions of that time have been distanced by what actually happened. I wanted only to escape, as if my life depended on it, but I had no reason then to suppose that it did.

But social reflexes are probably in the end more important than things on which one's life may depend. What could I do when I heard her calling me like that: in such accents of joy and, yes, anticipation.

Nancy came hastening towards me over the sunlit square. Her little face positively shone. She wore a very English sort of floppy cotton sunhat, elegant pale brown linen trousers and a silk shirt. She was carrying an expensively feminine handbag.

I said she only once called me Roland, which is not quite true, although it is true that she hardly ever used my name, and it was somehow memorable when she did. This must have been the last time.

Transformed yet again as she was, there was still something oldfashioned and even quaint about her, as if she were an older actress taking on a youthful part in TV. The way she had twice shouted out my name reminded me of an aunt of mine who bore a striking resemblance to Aunt Dahlia in the novels of P.G. Wodehouse: the one who orders Bertie Wooster about, and is at once querulous and self-assured, authoritative and yet calmly benevolent.

And so, all thoughts of escape gone, I found myself obediently waiting for Nancy, as she hurried over the square.

She didn't embrace or kiss me, as I half expected, but pulled me with a gesture of affection and abandonment towards the car.

'Come on, let's go,' she said. 'I've changed my mind. I'm going to leave everything and go with you right now. Never mind about Marseille. We'll drive to Paris and stay in some lovely hotel on the way.'

She'd had a thorough wash, no doubt about it. And she reeked now of perfume. 'Nancy,' I said, with an attempt at being authoritative myself. 'You must tell me exactly what's happened. What about your husband?' I went on, determined to hold her to her own story. 'Isn't he coming back? Is he still away? You can't just go rushing off with me you know' – and it was on the tip of my tongue to add, 'Even if I wanted to go away with you, which I don't.'

And yet I must admit that I felt increasingly not too sure about that. A kind of excitement to match Nancy's was rising in me. The notion of tearing off up France with her didn't seem such an extravagant one after all. In fact it began to appear rather glorious and liberating, as much unlike me as Nancy this morning was unlike her previous self.

But as we got in the car I still persisted. 'Has he, your husband, come back so that you can take a holiday yourself?' I asked.

It sounded feeble, but it was the best I could do to seem to go along with Nancy's story, to stimulate her into some other tale which fitted the present situation, whatever that was. Did she really want a walk-out with me? I could hardly help being gratified at the idea, however little I thought I wanted it myself.

She turned to face me in the car. Her eyes were shining.

'I'm free,' she said. 'He's left me. I had a phone call this morning. He's gone off with a woman in Tel Aviv.'

Well, that was just as convincing as the story that she was married to an agent in the Israeli security service, and that she sometimes did work on his behalf.

I felt there was no point in asking any more. If Nancy was free I was free too – free of all the puzzles about her, and my own speculations about what I should do. We were going away together. Free as the birds, as she had said in her letter.

I found myself driving rather fast. We were heading out of Mouriez, in a more or less northerly direction. There would be plenty of time to think about how we should get on to the autoroute.

'Stop!' she commanded suddenly.

We were going along a narrow road, hardly more than a track, which wound between pine trees and stony little overgrown valleys with a few half dead-looking orchard trees, olives, and apricots with black twisted boughs. All round us the Alpilles stuck up their miniature peaks of limestone, rising out of a dense scrub of *maquis*. It was a very picturesque place, certainly.

Nancy sprung out of the car, turned round and beckoned me. There was no parking problem. The sides of the little road merged into a smooth hard carpet of pine needles.

Nancy was off already into this wilderness, and I had no choice but to follow her. I suddenly had the disturbing feeling that it was here she had really decided to go, rather than to Paris. It was hot, and very still and silent. A jay or magpie screamed somewhere in the wood, and I saw a sudden flash of its wings.

Somehow we wriggled our way downhill, through a dense brake of brambles and tall green canes like bamboos almost, with big floppy leaves. I could see that Nancy already had a number of tears in her thin smart trousers. Mine were fortunately made of a more robust material. She seemed to have no clothes or suitcase with her. Perhaps she intended to buy something in Paris, if we ever got there.

The canebrake stopped abruptly. There was a melodious sound of water, flowing rapidly along. Hidden among the dense growth there appeared an elegant stone bridge: or rather, as I could now see since we were looking down on it, a stone aqueduct, through which greyish-green water was tumultuously pouring.

'The agricultural,' said Nancy simply, turning her face back towards me.

I got the general idea. It must be a kind of canal, fast flowing here in the precipitous country, bringing water to these secluded and now neglected orchards from the river Durance and the Basses Alpes. The brilliant autumn day disclosed a hidden water garden, at the point where the stone aqueduct traversed a deep gully, luxuriant with the green canes that made a winter break against the *mistral*.

We might have been in Poussin's Arcadia; and yet there was something sinister about it too, and in the silence almost expectant, as if our solitude could not remain undisturbed for long.

It was complete enough at the moment. The murmur of the water, fast flowing between its incongruously elegant stone embankments, had a tranquillising effect; and for the first time that day I had a sensation of peace, even of happiness. I no longer cared what we did, or where we went. Nancy, I could see, appeared to be feeling the same. For a moment I wondered what on earth was going on now in that head of hers, which had created so many inventions; and I was touched that she had brought me to a real place, her own place as it were, which she discovered and loved, and now revealed to me. Without thinking I slipped my arm through hers and I felt her return the pressure.

'I used to come here in the summer. The water's less than three feet deep, and it's very very cold, but it was heavenly in the really hot weather.'

As she spoke there was a disturbance in the smooth volume of the stream as it came swirling round a bend towards us. Some creature was struggling in the flow. As it came nearly abreast of us I saw what it was – a big lizard nearly two feet long and coloured a wonderful tint of bronze, with a bluish-green sheen. The colours shone on the wet scales as the lizard moved its short paws feebly and awkwardly. It found itself in a medium in which, for all its agility, it could do nothing.

How had it come to be there? It must have fallen in when negotiating the steep bank, and the force of the water had instantly carried it away.

'Oh!' said Nancy, pointing. Her face looked horrified.

I had the strange feeling that at last something had happened to her that could not be turned into instant fantasy, as she had turned those pictures at the Hague, making them start to work for her and suggest imaginary excitements.

'Quick, quick! Please! Oh help it!'

Easier said than done. The lizard had already been carried a few feet beyond where we were standing, but at that moment it came in contact with the abutment of the aqueduct bridge, where the water folded itself round the stone edge in a smooth pulsating crease. A few stick and debris were held there, and the creature too seemed to find a hold, at least momentarily.

'Help it! *Do help it!*'

Of course the place where it had been carried would have to be on the other side; and I could see no way over. The canal – the 'agricultural' as Nancy had called it, no doubt anglicising the local term – was about ten feet wide.

There seemed nothing for it. Should I kick off my shoes? – but I didn't know what the bottom was like, and it didn't occur to me to remove my trousers, perhaps because Nancy was beside me.

The water was colder than I would have thought possible, and swirled strongly round and, as it seemed, through me, over the crotch. I plunged across, screaming involuntarily with the shock of it, and the current surged, loud and discordant now as well as powerful. The beast was still there, still hanging on, perhaps only by virtue of the strong current pressing it against the stonework. It had no chance, obviously, of running up that stone out of the water, as it would have run up a wall on dry land.

Standing beside it, and keeping my balance with difficulty, I gingerly reached out a hand. How beautiful it was! The blues and greens in its fine scales gleamed in the sunlight, and I could see its small expressionless reddish eye. A forked black tongue leaped out once or twice, as if to show its distress, and I wondered if the magnificent creature – I could see now just how big it was – might also be poisonous, like a snake, or if it would bite.

Nancy was shouting something from the other bank but I paid her no attention. I seized the lizard round the waist, if lizards could be said to have a waist, while steadying myself against the stonework with my other hand. For a moment I seemed to hold it securely, and I was planning to throw it up and on to the bank: that seemed the best course both for itself and for me; but suddenly it began to wriggle so violently that I could no more hold it than I could have held an eel. Regardless of the water it wanted only to escape from me.

And it did. As if it had been a fish it was back in the water and at once almost out of sight, carried swiftly round the next bend. There was no chance of my going after it, though I was aware that Nancy was attempting to do so, running madly along the stone coping at imminent risk of falling in, until she was brought to a complete stop by the dense growth of gorse and brambles and tangled young cypresses. The stream plunged into this as if into a tunnel.

We had lost the battle for the creature's life. It would drown in a few minutes in the swift current, between the canal walls. So numb that I was almost unaware of the cold now I stood dejectedly in the water while Nancy walked slowly back along the bank, her trousers practically torn to ribbons by this latest encounter with the *maquis*.

I had failed. Could I have done it any better? Nancy knew I had failed. And whatever we had been going to do, like going off together, now seemed pointless, I think, to both of us.

It occurred to me briefly to regret her impulse to stop when we passed this wild place on the road. Had we not done so we might have been nearly at Orange by now, bound for Paris.

The way to the road seemed even more prickly and impossible than when we had come down, and being uphill it took twice as long. My soaking trousers felt heavy as lead. Neither of us said anything. Our high spirits, or at least the joyous impulse of liberation Nancy claimed earlier that morning, had received a jolt from which they seemed hardly likely to recover in the course of the day. In the meantime I supposed we must decide to do something, or go somewhere.

There was a man standing beside the car, a tall figure dressed in black. With some apprehension, even at that discouraged moment, I thought he must be the owner of the property, waiting to complain to us about the trespass, and the car parked on his land. Even in such a wild area as this one his rights were probably jealously guarded by the *propriétaire*.

Nancy had halted abruptly beside me, and I heard the sharp intake of her breath. The man was waiting for us to come to him. He looked very tall, very dark. He had his hands in his pockets in a relaxed way, and under one arm he was holding something red and, as it were, bushy. Evidently this was not the *propriétaire*. I thought for a confused moment that it must be an official from the town, a gendarme perhaps, who had somehow been alerted to the presence in this area of poachers or intruders, and who had come hastily from some civic event which involved the wearing of ceremonial headgear. For the object under the man's arm bore, I could now see, had the appearance of an elaborate hat. A red hat.

Then I understood. In a split second, even as Nancy came to a stop with me beside her, I realised that every word she had written in her 'Letter', or spoken to me in Mouriez, must be absolutely true. She had written and spoken what was true; she had not fantasised at all. Perhaps not even about her kidnapping at the restaurant. This man in front of us, whom I now saw could only be her husband, was proof of the fact.

It seemed to me at that moment that the only lie told was his, not hers. He had told Nancy by telephone that he was leaving her. He had told her he was going away with a woman he had met in Tel Aviv. That had not been the case. For here he was.

In spite of the speed with which I seemed to grasp these things, they still tumbled clumsily over and over each other in my head. I was too stunned to have a proper sense of the logic of them, or to fill in the details. Was that why I didn't instantly recall the moment at the end of Nancy's letter when her mysterious man had given her the red hat – a real one this time – as a supreme token of courtship and possession? Was it why, although Nancy had halted so abruptly, I continued for a moment to walk on towards the man who was standing by the car.

Whether this was so or not Nancy soon stopped me. She ran and gripped me, not by the arm but round the waist. In so doing she swung me round as well, by main force, and pushed me down the slope we had just climbed up. Her face was as white as paper, and something about it awed me, for it no longer bore any resemblance at all to the slightly comical and spirited 'Nancy' face that had emerged for me from her letter, and no resemblance either to her features as I had known them here in Mouriez. It seemed, literally, a death-face, and it struck me simultaneously and for the first time that Mouriez was a word like *mourir* – to die: the village must have got its name from some plague or massacre in the past.

No actual time ever seems needed for such reflections. The man was still standing by the car, with the hat under his arm; but as I recovered from the push Nancy had given me, and turned my head back, I saw that he was running towards us – towards me. And I saw his face: which is why I knew beyond any doubt that it was at me he was running.

Panic – a visitation of the God Pan, who killed the wild creàtures he caught with his bare hands – seems suited to that landscape. I ran down the hill, making, like a rabbit, for cover. I had one glimpse of Nancy and the man locked together in what seemed to be a violent struggle, and then I got into the thick bushes around which Nancy and I had tried to pick our way as we came down. I didn't try to pick any way now – on the contrary. I was down on my hands and knees, then flat on my face, wriggling under gorse bushes and between dense green junipers which were even more prickly, unbelievably prickly.

As I wriggled I could hear him coming after me, crashing about among the bushes. He was still on his feet of course.

I thought of the lizard, now dead. It would have trickled its agile way through places as thick or thicker than this, sometimes motionless except for the movement of its black forked tongue, on the look out for prey: insects, mice, the eggs of birds. Its beautiful colours would blend with the reddish earth, the spines and grey-blue flowers of rosemary. I invoked its powers most earnestly, and its protection. I had tried, I had done my best, to save it.

The crackling sounds pursued me. Wherever the bush was thickest I crawled into it, now in one direction, now in another, down the hill. The sounds seemed to get no nearer; then they stopped. The man must be listening. I lay motionless on my face: it was the thickest part I had come to. My face and shut eyes were scratched by dead brambles and live ones held my hair and clothes at the back of my neck. I could move no further.

The stillness continued. In it I began to hear, faintly, the sound of water. I must have managed to come quite a long way; I was close to the hidden aqueduct and the canal, the glimpse Nancy had given me of Arcadia.

Where was she now? Surely the man, her husband, would not have hurt her? It had been me he was after. And still was.

I lay still, my eyes closed against the brambles which were scratching my mouth and nose. I was completely exhausted. After what seemed an age I heard the sounds the man had been making begin again. They seemed to be going away. Presently all was quiet.

I went on lying there in a trance: it must have been for a long time. The adrenalin of fright, pumped out in my head-long flight, slowly dispersed I suppose. I think I slept, or at least became unconscious. When I woke all was quiet. A little wind had got up, sighing in the thicket and the grasses. A faint monotonous sound of water seemed to swell and diminish within it.

My first thought was that he might be still there, lurking motionless somewhere quite close by, waiting for me. But if so I saw there was nothing I could do about it. I could not lie there indefinitely. If he was clever he would wait till I had fully exposed myself, until he could see me cautiously making my way back up the hill.

I thought I could not possibly move forward, but I did. With infinite pain and labour I crawled on, down the hill. The noise of the canal grew louder, but I could see nothing. At any moment I might fall face forward into the bloody thing, like the lizard.

Suddenly it was under my nose. I rolled into it with difficulty and then managed to stand more or less upright. I was well hidden. The *maquis* grew with a kind of mad density where it could get some of the water, the bushes struggling and jostling one another. I turned myself upstream; I should have lost my balance at once if I had tried to wade down.

Now I made good progress, and quietly. At last when I came to a chute or waterfall which would have been too tricky to negotiate, I managed to get out. The banks were clearer here. I went obliquely up a hill, well screened with pine trees above clumps of gorse and juniper round which I still had to find a way. I soon lost all sense of direction. I had no idea any more of where the canal ran, but made my way on blindly. There was no sign at all of the road.

A woodpecker startled me with its mechanical laughter, and I saw it in flight, dipping between the trees. The air was still, and the sun quite hot enough to begin to dry me. I was panting and sweating from my exertions but I had no inclination to slow down. The heat made the resinous tang of the pines almost overpowering, and there was something animal in it which reminded me of that day in the car with Nancy – it already seemed long ago – and her all too evident obedience to her husband's command that she shouldn't wash.

Smell memories are vivid, and this one made both Nancy and her husband seem present all around me in the wood. What she had said in the car had seemed grotesque at the time, but of course she had been speaking the truth about that, as about everything else. The man who had hunted me, perhaps still was hunting me, would no doubt have tastes as feral as his emotions seemed to be.

Poor Nancy – what a fate. In the midst of my own troubles and my deadly fear of the man I had seen, and heard crashing about in pursuit of me, I spared a thought for this incomprehensible girl on whose behalf I had come to Mouriez. Now she had saved me, as I had failed to save the lizard.

And was she so incomprehensible? Perhaps she was no odder than anyone else? Her oddity had imposed itself on the world, at least on the world of her friends Cloe and

Charles, when she'd first had the whim, although probably not for the first time, of writing down what was happening to her. Had she made such things happen by the desire to write them? And did she write for her own pleasure, or to have a dig at Cloe? Both no doubt. Perhaps again, what had begun as pleasure, for her early pages were so full of insouciant *joie de vivre*, even if of a narcissistic kind, had turned at last into a more purposeful wish to discompose her friend: indeed to get revenge on her.

So had Nancy become odd, or strange or peculiar or whatever one called it, because of what she had written down about herself? Rather in the same way that people in portraits become strange and unique to our eyes just by being painted. If the painting's good enough, that is: and I reminded myself again that I really must see what that Red Hat picture looked like, as soon as I got home.

If I ever did get home. I know I felt at that moment that I should never escape from being hunted like an animal in those woods near Mouriez. Nancy at least had the dignity of a fate. I just seemed to be subjected to some absurd and random law of accident, like that poor drowned lizard. I thought about such things rather wildly as I continued my painful progress through that impossible landscape. I kept looking back too, over my shoulder. Not that I expected to see him: in some way I still didn't believe in him, in spite of my terror. The terror seemed a panic all my own, and the country's, ever since the disappearance into death of that beautiful creature I had at least been trying to save.

I even began to wonder whether I could have been mistaken in thinking he was chasing me with murderous intent. Perhaps he had just wanted a chat? An explanation? Man to man. Or simply to meet me – a friend of his wife's? My head went round and round, and the words in Nancy's postcard to Cloe suddenly appeared in it. 'Don't forget me.' I shouldn't forget that lizard, I knew. But had I begun to want to forget Nancy, if I could?

172

There was no way I could start to do so at the moment. Quite the reverse. We'd started out that morning well before eleven. I'd no idea what the time was now; hours seemed to have passed. But perhaps not, because the hot sun was still nearly overhead. I was quite high up at that moment, with a clear view for once over a valley below, and suddenly the sun winked on a distant windscreen: a car was moving along an invisible road down there.

When I reached the road at last I couldn't be sure in which direction Mouriez was. I recognised nothing; and the road seemed bigger than the one we had previously been on. It was also frequented, at least from time to time. A 2CV came chugging along, and I automatically raised my hand. I asked the man which way Mouriez was and he said he was going there. The drive took us about five minutes.

My samaritan dropped me unsmiling in the main square and chugged off. He was singularly taciturn for a Provençal, and had made no comment on my damp and dishevelled appearance. He was not sinister, but he seemed to be a part of the now entirely alien and hostile world which surrounded me. I had no car and no suitcase. On the other hand my wallet and air ticket were still intact in my breast pocket; and after striving through that landscape under the hot sun I was at least no longer soaking wet.

I went into the café where Nancy and I had always met, and ordered a Cynar, and then another one. The disgusting drink, which now hardly seemed even alcoholic, was somehow in keeping with my general situation. What had I better do? There was probably some way I could get to Marseille airport, where I would have to tell them the car had been stolen. Clearly that was the case. Nancy and her husband would hardly have left it parked beside the road, after the man had given up trying to catch me. Where were they now?

I had begun to feel that I hardly cared. I felt sure, for some reason, that they were nowhere near where I was. Nancy and her now indisputable husband had vanished like

173

demons, into their mysterious world: still mysterious, however real it had turned out to be.

For the moment at least Nancy had ceased to be of any interest to me. I wanted out. Naturally enough perhaps. I kept thinking, none the less, of the glimpse I had seen of her struggling with her man, her 'policeman' as she had called him. She had been trying to deflect him? To help me, save me? Presumably. But now I was merely disgusted by the whole idea of them both: the whole business.

It was shock, I suppose. But there was something else as well. I felt sorry for her, of course, but that didn't stop me feeling repelled, and wanting to get away. I suppose most men don't care to look into the abyss of female sexual psychology. I knew I didn't. Nancy wanted to be enslaved. It looked as if she had found out in that odd hotel in the Hague that she wanted to be enslaved. She seemed to have duly enslaved herself. But no doubt she wanted to be as free as the birds too. The impulse of delight that had made her come away with me this morning was a perfectly genuine one, as genuine as everything else in her story.

Enslaved by a stranger, and a most unsuitable one? No doubt that was all part of the fun. Give me Cloe any day. She wanted things that a man could understand, even if, as in my case, he didn't particularly want to share them. I had just wanted Cloe herself, in bed, and she understood that quite well and was not having any. But at least we had known where we were.

Cloe considered me a wimp, as I was well aware. No doubt I was one too. Nancy had called me 'you naff person' in her letter. Because I hadn't believed her? That was what she wrote. And she had written that she was free; that she wanted me to take her home.

The morning now seemed days ago; but looking back on it as I sat in the café I could not but feel once again that Nancy's joy and liberation, even her wish to share them with me in Paris on the way home, had been as authentic as the

174

rest of her story had turned out to be. In her outlandish predicament Nancy had clutched at me, made use of me, and I was quite prepared for that. When she thought she was free she had really and touchingly wanted me, for however short a time, to share her freedom.

There was no decision about it. Of course she hadn't suddenly decided to take me as a lover. It was just that we should have been together, and she would have been a different person – clean, fresh and joyous. Anything might, and probably would, have followed from that.

If only we had not stopped at that fatal place on the wild road out of Mouriez, to visit Nancy's Arcadia! I had a brief vision of her there in the torrid summer time, sitting in the green canebreak by the sound of the water. The swift canal would have been as cold then as now; I had myself experienced its coldness. Sitting there, would Nancy have looked as she had looked when I had first seen her by the war memorial? – meek, vacant and resigned, a captive on parole? Had her husband ever accompanied her? I had not thought to ask that, but he had certainly known where to look for her on his return. If indeed he had ever really been away.

He had probably gone no further than the next village. If he really was an Israeli agent – and that now seemed just as plausible as everything else in Nancy's account – he had probably been using an accepted safe house, or rest house, which happened to be in the quiet little township of Mouriez. He had installed his new wife there: mewed her up, as a jealous Italian nobleman or Victorian husband might have done? But if Nancy really was his faithful partner in confidential activities she would not have needed to be under guard?

Teachers of English are all the same: we instinctively translate the little we know of life into the much more that we know of literature. A couplet from Keats came into my mind.

Keats probably got the idea from Coleridge, but his lines certainly described my imagination of Nancy, sitting in her own secret green chasm. Which turned out not to have been so secret. Perhaps her husband had always secretly followed her there? She had been, still was, a demon's slave rather than his mistress? There was nothing demonic about poor Nancy herself. And where were the pair of them now?

So I meditated over my third Cynar, and was disinclined to try to find out. I must look after myself instead. My watch seemed to have survived the water intact, and if so it was now five o'clock. I could not bear the thought of going back to the Hotel Roi René, and submitting to the surprise and pleasure which its elderly proprietor would certainly show at my predicament. '*Mais Monsieur alors? … et votre fiancée? Ah, le pauvre!*' etc. No, definitely not. I must find somewhere else, and I must get myself something to eat, for I was now ravenously hungry.

I had just summoned the waiter (and that once tricky task was nothing to me now) when I became aware of a woman approaching my little table. She was middle-aged, dark, very neat and self-sufficient in appearance. She was looking at me not enquiringly but as if she was quite well aware who I was and what I was doing, and I suddenly realised that she was the same woman whom I had seen coming out of the house to which I had followed Nancy: the woman who had passed me by in the street as if on her way to the shops.

She held out a note towards me, and murmured something that sounded both sympathetic and understanding. But she kept her eyes down, not looking at me directly, and as soon as I had taken the note she turned and walked neatly away. Standing up and holding the note I gazed at her back, but could not think of anything sensible to call after her.

No 'Dear Roland' this time.

Madame Brunet will bring this to our café. I hope you're there – I think you will be, must be. It's all going to be all right – don't worry. I'll be waiting for you at 11 O'Clock with the car. In the Rue Passerelle. You can't miss it – you may know it. It's dark and quiet, just behind the square. He's not here – so don't worry.

That was all: no signature. It was Nancy's handwriting, and I felt a sudden affection for it though I had seen only one other sample, apart from the corrections over the typing in her letter to Cloe. The writing reassured me: it was so like the part of her that I had come to feel close to: the jokey, comical, somehow innocent Nancy. I felt affection for the sprawling way she wrote '11 O'Clock' in great capitals as if it was very important to her, as indeed perhaps it was.

And to me too. I sat down again in the café chair, holding the note in front of me and reading it again and again. Then I put it quickly in my wallet together with her other letter.

I was on guard again. I looked round furtively. just as I had done in the woods. Madame Brunet had disappeared. Everything looked normal. Would I have recognised Nancy's husband if he had been strolling about, or sitting in a café like a harmless citizen. Hard to say, but I don't see why I should have done. I decided to get away from the square at once.

I remembered seeing a small motel on the outskirts of the village, an ugly forlorn little place on the road to Arles and Tarascon. That should do me. I walked there, paid for a room, and cleaned myself up as best I could. My clothes remained stiff with thorns and barbed bayonets from the gorse. There was plenty of time, so after my shower I lay down and tried to rest, hungry as I was. Of course I went instantly and heavily to sleep. It was quite dark when I woke up, I blundered over in a panic to the light switch, terrified that I might already have missed our appointment. I felt I could not have borne my failure to have saved Nancy now, as I had failed to save the lizard.

But it was only half-past eight. Bemused and fixated by what I had to do I was none the less aware of a feeling of annoyance, as I stumbled like a sleep-walker about the mean little room, at Nancy's saying 'so don't worry'. She had used the word twice. I wasn't worrying. I was going to grasp this second chance with both hands.

I walked back into Mouriez. I no longer felt tired, but my clothes, full of prickles, itched all over me. I hardly felt hungry now either. A proper evening meal would make me sleepy again, I knew, and I went into a cafeteria and had a sandwich and a glass of beer. Even that was difficult to get down. Excitement I suppose.

'So don't worry.' It was really most irritating of Nancy to repeat that. She thought me 'naff' (disgusting contemporary term), always timid and cautious, a typical English academic. I would not bother to show her that she was wrong – I didn't care about that – but I would prove that she could rely on me absolutely; that I was ready for whatever she wanted to do, whatever plan of escape she now had. If she indeed had one.

But I was sure she did. Even at eleven o'clock at night we could take the car and vanish into Provence without anyone knowing where we had gone. There had been no doubt that morning that she was longing to escape, and that only some malign chance had prevented it. I must – I simply must – now help her to get away, for good and all.

Of course Nancy was right – she was always right, just as I knew her now to be always truthful. She was right about me, and my character, and my instincts. Even at this moment I was quite well aware of a slight feeling of nostalgia – homesickness almost – for that horrible room back at the motel, where I had slept off this morning's physical and emotional exhaustion. Had taking that room, after I had already received Nancy's note, been a sign of my inherent preference for a cautious belt and braces policy? If she didn't turn up I could go back and get a good night's sleep, which

I felt I needed. I bought a couple of sandwiches before leaving the bar, and a plastic bottle of wine. With these in my pocket, I should have something to fall back on, one way or the other.

I already knew where Rue Passerelle was; I had after all been strolling around Mouriez on a daily basis for what seemed a long time now. But to be on the safe side I did a cautious reconnaissance when it was getting on for ten o'clock. It was a short quiet street, not going anywhere in particular, in the oldest part of the town. It was narrow, with tall old houses looking down from both sides. Of course there were cars in it, slewed about at all angles on and off the pavement, but there was no real parking problem. I imagined Nancy would be waiting somewhere near the open end of the street. The other was a near *impasse*.

I was wrong. There was no one about in the street at eleven o'clock. Small French towns go to bed early: even the bar I had been in was shut soon after ten. I came in by the narrow end, the one furthest from the square, and at once saw Nancy sitting in my little hired Renault, facing me.

She sprang out of the car and rushed towards me with her arms held out wide. I did the same. In the lamplight I could see her little face shining with joy; and I knew at once not only that this time we really would go away together, but that I loved her. After all that had happened it seemed as inevitable as the dawn or the sunset.

She fell into my arms. and I felt her small slight body trembling. She kissed me. Then she stood back, with her hands on my shoulders, and I saw suddenly that her face looked bruised, there was a purplish mark near one eye. I had barely time to register the horror of this when her face abruptly changed expression. It had real horror in it, as she threw her arms round my neck again, and shouted something. I must have been hit very hard on the back of the head. I was in the gutter, helpless and some dark creature was violently pushing and pulling me, hitting me too.

I must have lost consciousness, at least partly, although I had a confused awareness of a struggle going on, my clothes being ripped, things pulled out of them. This seemed to go on almost in silence though there were noises too – hoarse and heavy ones. I had the impression of a foot near my face, and small hands clutching it, so that my face remained unbroken; but to protect it I was squeezing it myself into the cool damp stone, where I felt it could relax and go to sleep.

I may have heard a car start up: I'm not sure.

*

The hospital at Tarascon was clean and spacious, and I had a white hood over my bed. Then they took it away and gave me eye tests, looking up and looking down, repeating letters and numbers in the regular pattern of a strobe light. The nurse told me she thought it was only a minor concussion; and presently the doctor told me so too. I formed the impression that the French like, if possible, to make an elegant little drama out of any medical scenario, in the tradition of their classic playwrights.

As an *anglais* I was probably a disappointment to them. I did not take the nurse's hand and murmur 'Where am I? – what has occurred?' or something of that sort. I knew quite well what had occurred: I knew a great deal more than they did. There seemed to be no point in talking about it, though I was perfectly well able to do so, even in French.

They said they would keep me under observation for a couple of days, as a precaution. Apart from an extreme soreness at the back of my head, which was bandaged, I felt perfectly normal, and even managed to eat some of the hospital food. No wine was provided.

On the second morning a competent-looking lady came to see me from the administration. She carried a plastic bag, sealed at the top with an official twist of paper. It contained my wallet and passport and everything else that had been in

180

my pockets, including my keys. And the key of the little hired Renault.

Apart from the sandwiches and the wine bottle only two other things were missing: the note that Madame Brunet had brought me and Nancy's letter and note to me. They had been in my wallet. I was lucky not to have been castrated I suppose. That thought did go through my sore head.

The competent lady said my suitcase was waiting for me downstairs, in her office. Did I require anything from it? No, I did not. And were there any phone calls she could make on my behalf, perhaps to relatives in England? They would have to charge me of course for such calls when I left the hospital. No, thank you. It was not necessary to call anyone.

One more thing. The ambulance crew who brought me in after my accident had, as a matter of routine, notified the police. An *agent* would like to see me briefly, at my convenience, before I left. Purely a formality.

Having ascertained delicately that I understood the French language, the *agent*, a neat young man in plain clothes, read me a short report based on that of the ambulance crew. A householder in Rue Passerelle had rung the emergency services at eleven-fifteen on Wednesday night. On his way home he had found a man lying outside his house in the gutter, apparently stunned. He was respectably dressed (the policeman assumed a slightly apologetic expression at this point), seemed conscious, but was barely able to speak. Evidently a foreigner. There was an ignition key in his hand, and also evidently he had just parked a small car, a metre or so *en face*. It seemed he had stumbled in the roadway and struck his head severely on the edge of the pavement.

The *agent* made an inquiry with his eyebrows. Had I any comment to make on the report.

No, really none at all. I had just parked my hired car, with a view to looking for a hotel in the neighbourhood, when I must have tripped and fallen over.

181

So if I had heard a car start it would not have been the little Renault, from which Nancy had sprung to embrace me.

*

No doubt it was the knock on the head, for I was not aware, when I left the hospital, of feeling any emotion at all. I didn't want to think about what had happened. At the time I was curious, in a dull sort of way. A local representative of the hire firm had been to see me, and I told him that if they brought the little car, or another, I would continue to hire it, paying of course for the days I had been immobilised, and hand the vehicle over at Marseille when I flew home. He seemed content with that arrangement.

I drove back to Mouriez. Very sore as it still was, my head was getting better, and was now unbandaged. I took an aspirin, a supply of which I always keep in my pocket. They had been returned to me at the hospital with my other possessions.

I knew – indeed I was quite sure – that Nancy and her husband would no longer be in Mouriez. But the feeling of dull curiosity made me want to go back, and I was not now in the least afraid to do so. I wanted to see again where Nancy had lived.

I drove into the village, past the square and on to the outskirts: the way I had driven with Nancy a few days before. There was the ugly little house, in its road devoid of trees. I turned into the road and stopped just beyond the house.

The outside shutters were up, but in France that need not mean a place is empty. However I knew it was empty. I got out of the car and strolled in the direction of the next house, one built to the same sort of pattern.

Private and secretive the place certainly was, and yet it all looked very peaceful. Mouriez was like that. Anything could have been going on, and probably was, but the proprieties

182

were fully observed. Nothing louche in the modern manner. No question of letting anything hang out. And the quiet streets safe by night. My *agent de police* had made some deprecating comment about the streets of London, where muggers were known to abound. London, or Marseille, I couldn't help adding. The French will get at you if they can, in their polite way. But the *agent* had every right to imply that what had happened to me in Mouriez could only have been an accident.

The woman of the next house was in her garden – a bit of luck. She glanced up at me while I affected to hesitate, looking around in uncertain fashion. Finally an 'Excusez-moi, Madame'. Did she know of an English couple, acquaintances of mine, whom I was hoping to look up? But yes, in that house, there, Monsieur. Foreigners. English, were they? She saw little of them, but she had spoken sometimes with their housekeeper, Madame Brunet.

From the way she spoke it was all in the past. I enquired about that. Yes, they had gone away, she thought. Madame Brunet had told her the house would shortly be up for sale. Madame herself was going to stay with friends in Poitiers, look for a suitable job there.

A child cried inside the house. The woman turned to her door with a gesture of apology. I turned to contemplate the other house, blank behind its shutters, and saw one of them opening. The face of Nancy appeared, with Madame Brunet standing watchfully behind her. For a split second I seemed to be sure of it: then I realised it must be some other young woman, and her mother, or someone from the estate agency, looking over the house. The shutter had closed again. The glimpse made Nancy's absence all the more complete.

And yet .... My own head was not quite right yet. I had a vision of Nancy's fantasies, as they had once seemed, as if I were now taking part in them myself. I must get away before something else happened. But was it really possible the three of them could still be inside the house, and that they had seen me?

My idea had been to stop the night somewhere nearby, perhaps make further enquiries. But I drove straight to Marseille airport and managed to get a booking home on the evening flight.

*

While I was in hospital I had toyed with the idea of telling Cloe nothing at all. How satisfactory to keep the whole business to myself. Or I could tell her a lot of lies. I felt resentment against Cloe on several counts. She had landed me in a lot of trouble: involved me in a tale which no longer concerned herself. It was Nancy and me who were the story-tellers now, linked indissolubly not so much in the bond of what had happened to us, but of what we had both written down; or, in my case, were shortly to write down. Nancy had written the truth, so it appeared, and so would I. But nothing written is ever really true. What was true was what had actually happened to Nancy: and I could not bear to think of that. But of course I had to.

Besides, and on a meaner level, I could hardly resist seeing what Cloe made of it all. What would she think of what I would tell her of Nancy's husband? Had she really spent the night with him after that *kermesse* dance at the Hague? – the rest of the night and most of the day after? Naturally I didn't expect to learn the truth about that from Cloe herself, but I was sure I would be able to deduce it from the way Cloe received my news.

But that was a trivial matter. Much more important was the incontrovertible proof – I could still feel it on the back of my head – that Nancy had told the truth about her man, and about what had happened to her as a result.

In her own story the 'policeman' she had fallen in love with had nearly strangled her: she had been frightened after-

184

wards but gratified at the time. She thought he hadn't meant it, and love and fear seem to have been at the heart of her infatuation. In her irrepressible way she had evidently thought it funny too: she had loved him for making her laugh.

But the Nancy I had first seen in Mouriez had not seemed exactly brimming with fun and games. And what might he have done to her after dealing with me that night?

In spite of what had happened what did I really know about it, even now? Perhaps she could manage him perfectly well most of the time? Perhaps he had it in him to become the kindest and most rational of husbands. Perhaps when they had a child ...?

Well, whatever I was feeling now, I would certainly suppress my own feelings when I spoke to Cloe.

I hardly knew what my feelings were in any case; but on the flight back to London I began to feel quite weak with delayed shock, or delayed emotion, or something worse than that. The thought of Nancy was simply too much, but it was there all the time, and a horrible lump at the back of my throat. Always a bit of a hypochondriac, I felt definitely concerned about myself. More so than about Nancy I suppose. The hospital in Tarascon could easily have been wrong, after all. I might find myself permanently injured by that blow on the head. My brain, or nervous system, or whatever it was, never the same again?

As the plane whistled over the Alpilles shortly after take-off – I could see them down below in the clear air, though I could not make out Mouriez itself – I had made a determined attempt to cheer myself up. I was free from it all now. I even tried to feel that Nancy herself might have colluded in her husband's attack on me. She, and Madame Brunet, might have set me up. By a strange paradox it was even comforting to feel that Nancy and her husband might have the solidarity of a married couple, planning things together, the wife humouring her husband's wishes, even when they were murderous ones.

Was that going too far? No doubt it was, but anything to escape from the torment of thinking what could have happened to Nancy, after my 'accident'. Let me at least hope that she hadn't really wanted to escape with me. Perhaps her behaviour had been simply wanton, even kinky. She had been pleasing herself with thoughts of further fake enslavement, when she 'confessed' to her husband what she had been up to. She may not have suspected how violent he could become. She may have been appalled by what happened?

But then again, perhaps not? I thought of the red thing, the red hat thing, that he seemed to have been carrying when I saw him that morning, standing by the car. Was that a kind of private sign, a pledge of their mutual understanding in any escapade, no matter how it might turn out? As I say, her letter shows that Nancy had plenty of freakish humour. She had fallen in love with her 'policeman' not only because he behaved so oddly, but because she found she loved to tease him about these oddities. Had these become the kind of games that a certain kind of young married couple liked to play? Had such games gone too far, through misunderstanding? Newly married couples often misunderstand each other: look at Othello and Desdemona.

Deep down, as I sat in the plane, I knew that such constructions and speculations bore no relation to the brutal facts. Nancy was not half of a married couple. She was virtually a slave: a slave who had wanted to escape. And had wanted me to help her. I remembered vividly, from the moment she had embraced me, the dark bruise I had seen on her cheek. What further price would she be paying now?

I would not talk about this to Cloe. I let three or four days go by before ringing her up. She was busy, and sounded more than usually cool and uninterested, but she asked herself to tea on the coming Saturday. Tea! – I ask you. She said it was the only free moment she had.

I told her a certain amount – not everything. I was jealous of whatever feelings I had for Nancy. I said nothing about our hidden Arcadia by the canal: nothing about our going away together. I was detached, quite clinical, interested as a man of my intelligence would be, but making it clear that I thought Nancy (and by imputation Cloe herself) were persons whose affairs need not be taken all that seriously. This had an immediate effect: Cloe became cross.

The crosser the better from my point of view. Anything but Cloe the cool. Seeing she was ruffled I pressed home my advantage. I pointed out that Nancy's Letter had told the whole truth about what had happened: that was the disturbing thing about it. So had she, Cloe, really gone off with this policeman after the ball? Had she even fallen for him a bit, as Nancy had suspected?

I asked the question neutrally but pointedly, like a counsel in court. And in the same spirit I waited for a reply.

Cloe didn't give me one, of course. Instead she managed to put me at an instant disadvantage: not a difficult thing to do in a relationship between Cloe and a man like myself.

She smiled and said hadn't we both agreed that Nancy's tale was all made up. Which being so, couldn't I see that the man she was living with in France had no connection at all with the stuff she had concocted about their trip to see the Vermeers at the Hague? I was making an obvious mistake, wasn't I, assuming that the Hague stuff must be true, because Nancy was living with a man in Mouriez, a man I had encountered in the flesh, so to speak?

'And your poor head,' she said, reaching a white hand tenderly in my direction; without it making contact with any part of me, however.

I could hardly have concealed that accident from Cloe, nor would I wish to have done so. My broken head had been acquired in her service, after all.

'It must have been a man she'd met in France,' Cloe went on. 'That must surely be obvious. Probably a Marseillais. They can be a pretty tough lot the French, especially in the south. The poor girl wouldn't have known what she was in for. I daresay it all started with another fantasy, like the one she'd written down.'

The awful thing was that at this point I began to waver myself. Back in London, with cool calm collected Cloe, the essential romance of the things that had happened to me, the emotions I had felt, began to wither away. Perhaps she was right? I saw myself that I had still no idea who the man was. He could have been a citizen of Mouriez, or a tough guy from Marseille, though I resented Cloe's bogus air of expertise about such persons. He could even have been the landowner or farmer to whom the wild country of Nancy's Arcadia belonged. A man she'd encountered there, a masterful and a jealous man?

But in that case why did she stop and take me with her into the creature's lair? Certainly I could see that the whole mystery of Nancy's behaviour was no nearer being solved, and in view of Cloe's brisk matter-of-factness that was some kind of comfort to me. At the same time I remembered my own doubts about what Nancy had told me of her 'marriage', and her work with or for her husband in European capitals – doubts which had suddenly been dissipated by the apparition of the tall man in dark clothes, standing beside the car. I saw now that it had been naive of me to assume instantly, and in the heat of the moment, that the sensational appearance of this man made Nancy's whole tale a true one.

'Perhaps she is married at that,' Cloe was saying. 'Perhaps Madame Brunet is her mother-in-law. In one way I can believe anything of dear old Nance.'

I detested her tone. 'Nancy is in trouble,' I said flatly. 'There can hardly be any doubt about that. She's gone away, or been taken away. There can't be any doubt about that either. If I'd seen her again I'd have tried to help her. But she's gone away.'

My attempt to counter Cloe's casual tone did not sound convincing, even to me. It sounded feeble, and all the feebler from trying to strike the note of conscience and concern.

'Poor Nancy,' Cloe was going comfortably on, taking no notice. 'Charles always thought of her as a boy. I daresay down in France she was trying too hard to be a woman. To show she could. Female masochism you know. And, Roland dear, come off it. You become more and more like yourself every time I see you.'

'Well, she wrote to you "Don't forget me," and I certainly shan't forget her. We'll probably never see her again.'

I was sounding worse and worse now, and Cloe seemed to recognise that by simply smiling and saying nothing. Without being invited she poured herself out another cup of tea.

At that moment something occurred to me – why hadn't I thought of it before? The back of my head was aching now and I was disliking Cloe more and more by the minute, but there was a piece of evidence which I'd wholly forgotten, and which now struck me with great force. It was the red hat. Surely I had seen this object – a floppy furry red thing – under the arm of the man who stood by the car? Surely it was, *must* be, the hat which her mysterious policeman had presented to Nancy as they left the hotel. Cloe had herself gone red, she wrote, at that moment, and looked thoroughly put out.

Of course it *could* have been just some red object. By why should he have been carrying a red object? Frenchmen don't walk about with red things under their arms.

He was bringing his wife her hat. The hat he had originally given her. The hat which had become, perhaps, a pledge of her servitude to him, in all sorts of different places.

So I thought, of course pretty wildly, but Cloe's attitude had made me so cross. I had become the hot and bothered one now, not Cloe. But I made a great effort, and tried to answer her smiling silence with a silence of my own. If I had proof, at least in some degree, that Nancy's story was true; and that Cloe was a liar, at least by implication, I resolved to say nothing about it.

We finished our tea almost in silence. I thought Cloe looked at me a little anxiously from time to time. Did she guess I was keeping something back, which I might have revealed if she had played her cards differently? I didn't care what she thought. Nancy was my own affair now, and in my own sense my own possession.

But I wasn't going to leave it quite there. Maybe there is nothing so impenetrable as a pretty self-confident womanly woman, but I could try my hand at being enigmatic too. Also, I hoped, a trifle disturbing.

'You did make the red hat for Nancy,' I told her, just as she was leaving. 'And everything seems to have followed from that.'

Cloe turned on the stairs and blew me a kiss. I was about to shut my door when she paused, and in typical Cloe fashion managed to have the last word.

'You fell for her a bit yourself, didn't you?'

What she meant, I knew, was that I had fallen for a dream figure. And so she classed me in her own estimation with Nancy, who had fallen for one too.

*

I really thought that was the end of it. But in less than a week Cloe rang me up.

'Nancy telephoned this morning,' she announced. 'From Paris. She's coming over in a few days' time.'

Stupefaction. What was there to say? I said nothing. Cloe took no notice of that but just burbled on comfortably.

'I'm hoping she'll be here for the wedding,' she told me. 'She'll need a bit of looking after too, and she can stay at my place for a few days. She'll be a help getting all my stuff ready.'

For a sickening moment I could imagine Nancy undergoing this new form of imprisonment. Cloe's handmaid. Charles dropping in every evening, and chat about the honeymoon.

'Is she bringing her boyfriend?' I managed to get out. Rather pointed, I thought, in the circumstances. The banality of the word seemed suited to this new image of how things would be.

'Oh no,' went on Cloe, even more comfortably. 'That's all over I gather.'

Well: why shouldn't it be?

A really ghastly depression overwhelmed me. It must be caused by the fact that Nancy was alive and well and coming to England, and was just like everybody else. Certainly not like the girl I had made for myself in Mouriez, the strange little captive who had longed to escape with me. I wanted my own Nancy back I suppose. The girl who had written about the Girl with the Red Hat. (I still haven't seen a picture of that picture, and I'm not sure now that I want to.)

'When she arrives you'll come and see us, won't you, Roland?' Cloe was saying. 'What a surprise it will be for her. The nice man she met in Mouriez turning out to be a friend of the family, as it were.'

Yes, it would be a surprise. And it was one I did not propose to give Nancy. Or myself for that matter. What could we talk about? How she had escaped? But probably she hadn't escaped; she was going back cheerfully into bondage. Perhaps the man who had attacked me was quite content to let her go: knowing that she would come back to him.

Who *was* he, this man? I suspected that Cloe wouldn't even ask, wouldn't really want to know, whatever Nancy might try to tell her. For Cloe it was 'all over'. It would be all a bit of nonsense in the past, even if Cloe herself had once been involved with him, this man. And I couldn't ask, because I wouldn't be going to see Nancy. I feel quite sure about that.

Nancy doesn't even know my surname, let alone my address and telephone number. Unless, of course, she opened my passport, and collaborated in the search of my wallet. But all that doesn't matter. It is to Cloe's unmotherly arms that she will turn now when she comes to England, and Cloe will have to hear all about her adventures.

But if she really does appear, and if Cloe should ring me up, I shall go round I expect. Merely out of curiosity; and to ask, if we should get a moment to ourselves, what became of the red hat.

Can I do this without admitting that I knew about the red hat all along? Yes: for now that Nancy seems about to be taken over by Cloe I can tell her that Cloe once mentioned it to me.

But no; on second thoughts I shall say nothing about it, nothing at all. Whatever there has been between Nancy and me can stay as it is, out of Cloe's reach. And in fact, if Nancy does come, I'm sure Cloe will keep it quiet, and not ask me round at all. She won't be able to resist hearing all about me from Nancy, and revealing that she already knows me would spoil that. She'll just say afterwards that Nancy couldn't stay – had to get back to France.

Nancy will turn to Cloe and be made use of. But I don't think she'll be at Cloe's wedding. I hope not, because of course I shall have to go to it myself. As an old friend: and out of curiosity.